The Phantom of Thomas Hardy

The Phantom of

Thomas Hardy

A novel by

Floyd Skloot

The University of Wisconsin Press

The University of Wisconsin Press
1930 Monroe Street, 3rd Floor
Madison, Wisconsin 53711-2059
uwpress.wisc.edu

3 Henrietta Street, Covent Garden
London WC2E 8LU, United Kingdom
eurospanbookstore.com

Printed in the United States of America

This book may be available in a digital edition.

Library of Congress Cataloging-in-Publication Data

Names: Skloot, Floyd, author.
Title: The phantom of Thomas Hardy / Floyd Skloot.
Description: Madison, Wisconsin: The University of Wisconsin Press, [2016]
Identifiers: LCCN 2016013570 | ISBN 9780299310400 (cloth: alk. paper)
Subjects: LCSH: Hardy, Thomas, 1840–1928—Fiction.
Classification: LCC PS3569.K577 P47 2016 | DDC 813/.54—dc23
LC record available at https://lccn.loc.gov/2016013570

For

Beverly

"For winning love we win the risk of losing,
And losing love is as one's life were riven."

Thomas Hardy, "Revulsion"

"That her fond phantom lingers there
Is known only to me."

Thomas Hardy, "Memory and I"

"Time unveils sorrows and secrets."

Thomas Hardy, "The Flirt's Tragedy"

"Things and events always were, are, and will be
(e.g., Emma, Mother and Father are living still in
the past)."

Thomas Hardy's diary,
June 10, 1923, a week after his eighty-third birthday

A Note to the Reader

Though characters and events in this novel resemble those in my life, most are entirely creations of the imagination. In such cases, any resemblance to real characters and events is purely coincidental. After publishing four memoirs in which I never got to make anything up, writing this fictional memoir was something else entirely, which was the point.

Thomas Hardy had his own oddball approach to presenting his life story: the self-ghostwritten biography. As an old man, he composed his memoirs and instructed his wife to publish them after his death as though they were a biography she herself had written. So *The Early Life of Thomas Hardy, 1840–1891* and *The Later Years of Thomas Hardy, 1892–1928* were duly published under Florence Hardy's name in 1928 and 1930. The ruse didn't fool many readers. Despite the profound gaps, evasions, and misdirections of those memoirs, and despite the burning of his papers, Hardy failed to discourage interest and scrutiny into his life. Instead, he called attention to the fact that there was much he wished to hide.

The Phantom of Thomas Hardy

Beverly and I walked up South Street in Dorchester, following a tourist map past Trespass Outdoor Clothing, Carphone Warehouse, Top Drawer Cards & Gifts, a shuttered O2 Store. All the bold signage and trendy commercial space made the street feel very twenty-first-century England. But above storefront level, the nineteenth-century world of Thomas Hardy was present in the worn masonry of squat, flat-topped buildings huddled together, their severe faces brightened by an occasional bow window.

It was Monday, June 4, 2012. We'd been touring England for two weeks, driven 1,377 miles from London to Oxford to Wales to Cornwall and finally to the place I'd hoped to visit for the last forty-four years, ever since I was a college senior immersed in Hardy's novels. I'd come to honor the bond I felt with both Hardy and the teacher who'd led me to his work.

After last night's Queen's Jubilee party in Dorchester Borough Gardens, the old county town was quiet that morning, rain gone but heavy clouds still lurking. Back home in Portland, Oregon, the full strawberry moon as it set was being swallowed by a predawn partial eclipse. Just as this thought occurred, and with it the sense that Time was off-kilter at the moment, I felt something brush my shoulder.

I ignored it, figuring a passerby had grazed me because we'd stopped abruptly. Beverly raised our joined hands and pointed them at a building set back a few feet from the others. "Oh look, Floyd."

There at 10 South Street, beside the heavy wooden door of a Barclays Bank, we saw a round blue plaque: "This house is reputed to have been lived in by the MAYOR of CASTERBRIDGE in THOMAS HARDY'S story of that name written in 1885."

The building still appeared as Hardy had described it in the novel, faced with dull red-and-gray old brick, its small paned Georgian sash windows enlivened with three coats of white. Once past the notion of the place as a bank, I could imagine its interior appointed to profusion with heavy mahogany furniture of the deepest red-Spanish hues, its large lofty rooms, the chimneypiece intricately carved with garlanded lyres and ox skulls. That an actual building was being proclaimed as the home of a fictional character made it seem like the perfect gateway for our visit, a mystical spot that linked Hardy's real and imagined worlds.

I walked over to stand beneath the blue plaque and posed for a photo. Cross-legged, back resting against the bank's night safe, I beamed at Beverly, filled with love for her, gratitude that she took this journey with me, delight at being there. We planned to go to Hardy's birthplace at Bockhampton next, then over the final two days of our travels we would visit his home at Max Gate, the gravesite at Stinsford Churchyard where his heart is buried, and the landscape of the region he called Wessex. I thought of this as a kind of homecoming to a place I'd never been, only known through books and poems, films, dreams.

After I returned to her side, Beverly raised the camera to take a photo of the building without me in front of it. The wind rose, the chill making me zip up my vest.

That's when I felt another glancing contact against my shoulder, followed this time by an unmistakable, firm tap. What I thought was the wind spoke into my ear: "Something I missed."

There was no doubt I'd heard it. Three distinct words. Nor was there doubt about whose voice had spoken, gentle, level, refined, precisely modulated, just as it was said to have been by his contemporaries. A soft-cadenced voice with a faint suggestion of rough rustic flavor in it, according to an acquaintance of Hardy's who sounds like he's describing red wine.

"Something I missed," Thomas Hardy said to me.

≋

When I spun around, Hardy was gone. But he was also not gone, not quite, and the first thing that registered for me was the lingering physical impression of his touch, a sense memory still palpable at my shoulder. The breeze contained a fading echo of his final word. This man who never liked to touch or be touched had touched me twice. This private, secretive soul, a formal and socially cautious spirit, had made contact, had spoken. And now that he had my attention, Hardy was withdrawing.

Beverly snapped a photo of me then, one of the candid shots she loves to take from about three feet away. They often end up on my website or Facebook page or book covers because she has a knack for seeing right into me, for capturing me at my most open. I'm standing there, face in profile, looking confused as I gaze toward the Marks & Spencer store window, right hand raised to my left shoulder joint.

She let the camera dangle from her neck and studied me, worried, having recognized something in my face. "Let's rest for a minute," she said, and headed to a bench a few yards up the street.

Before I sat, I looked around for any trace of Hardy. It was difficult to concentrate. I tried to focus full attention on each individual I saw but it was a struggle to sort through the comings and goings. A tall man in a white vest and straw hat limped past our bench, hands clasped behind his back, listing left as he spoke to a woman half his size. Clearly not Hardy. Two middle-aged men, both far too bulky to be Hardy, stood with their heads cocked and arms akimbo, studying the display of shoes in Stead & Simpson's window. Twins, I'd guess. At 39 South Street, a few doors down and on the opposite side of the street, was the Gorge Cafe, an establishment featuring breakfast-all-day and brewed coffee.

This was the building where Hardy at sixteen had begun his training as an architect, apprenticed to the esteemed John Hicks. Hicks had often hired Hardy's father, a mason, to work on church restorations, so this was a place the family knew well. Below the window was a sign saying "Great food is our pleasure" and below that was another sign saying "Even Thomas Hardy would be delighted." As I watched, a teenager drifted out of the Gorge and my heart quickened. But the boy flipped his hoodie over his head, checked his cell phone, and walked away. I turned to glance again at the mayor's house. Two buildings north, directly across from the bench, I saw Hardy's face. Faded and sketchy, it seemed to flicker there at the edge of sight. Then I realized what I was seeing. In a window of the WHSmith bookshop there was a sun-bleached sign with Hardy's visage looming above the covers of his most popular novels, on sale three for the price of two. Most of the glass storefront was doorway and a breeze rippled the sign.

I took a deep breath and sat beside Beverly. Just being there close to her calmed me. We leaned together over her camera's monitor to look at the South Street photos she'd taken in the last few minutes: the town pump, the narrow Antelope Walk alleyway, storefronts, the mayor's house. The close-up of me taken just after Hardy had touched my shoulder was weird, slightly blurred in a way Beverly's photos seldom are, as though autofocus had sensed a point of interest a few feet beyond me. The hazy, misty weather added a dimension of otherworldliness to the image. It could not have been a more accurate representation of my state of mind at that moment.

꧁

I should probably mention something here. Over the last two decades, I'd had a few episodes that we called Visitations.

They began during the years when Beverly and I lived in the middle of twenty acres of woods, in a small cedar yurt she'd built on a hillside in rural western Oregon. The ground was hard basalt from old lava flows, part of a dark crystalline column almost a thousand feet thick. It wasn't water-friendly land up on the hill, and it had been invaded by poison oak and wild blackberry, and on windy nights we thought the old oaks and evergreen would crash down on us. But despite its harshnesses this was the landscape of happiness for me. Living there taught me that paradise is approximate and never what we imagine it to be. We lived there together for thirteen years, a few miles outside a tiny town named Amity, and we loved the quiet, the isolation. Our nearest neighbor, a winery whose owners didn't live onsite, was more than a quarter mile away. Days would pass without our seeing another person.

In the silence on our land, occasionally I'd detect movement among the oak to our east that was different from the way deer or skunks or raccoons moved through the space. Or an unfamiliar shape would be illuminated deep in the woods when late-afternoon light found its way through the swaying canopy of Douglas fir. Keeping still, watching, I'd realize the deer was Paul Gauguin wearing a saffron-colored shirt, with a fringe of hair dangling where I thought I'd seen leaves. He was furious, radiating rage at having found himself in a different sort of paradise from the one he'd always yearned for. He stalked along the hill's crest till he reached a lush thicket of color, lilac and lily and bleeding heart, then surrendered to its embrace. Or the flash of light would clarify as Johann Sebastian Bach standing in a tangle of vines and upheaved stones, his arms raised as he conducted darkness down, finding beauty and harmony within the confusion and apparent havoc around him.

Sometimes familiar shapes or movements were not what I took them to be. I'd catch glimpses of a buck's antlers drifting west to east through the mist across the hill's crest and realize after a while what I was seeing wasn't antlers at all. In that particular case, it turned out I was seeing Vladimir Nabokov stalk a spring azure butterfly near our blueberry bushes. He was blind to me but rapt in noticing everything else, a lesson in itself. Once, shortly after our first well went dry, as I sat in a cracked Adirondack chair under twin fir and waited for a late afternoon dose of analgesic to kick in, I saw an oak branch sway and realized, no, it was an umbrella floating through a clear spot where there was an abandoned beehive. I thought an umbrella would be the last thing anyone would need in our drought-stricken county. Then I saw that the umbrella was actually a bowler hat, and it was resting on the head of T. S. Eliot, Mr. Waste Land himself, who was muttering about dry months and rock and no water.

I know how this sounds, how strange it seems. But sane people are known to have hallucinations. Oliver Sacks—in a book, not a Visitation—said that more than 10 percent of normal people in normal circumstances experience hallucinations. In the newest edition of the *Diagnostic and Statistical Manual of Mental Disorders*, the *DSM-5*, hallucinations are recognized as perfectly normal phenomena. Phantoms appear, and as Sacks says, "the feeling that someone is there, to the left or the right, perhaps just behind us, is known to us all." It's even more common in unfamiliar surroundings. A person hears voices, sees figures move, smells odors.

For me, however, these Visitations went beyond the hallucinatory because they had content, had depth. They seemed intended to teach me, and sometimes the Visitor too, something essential. The great Brooklyn Dodgers shortstop Pee Wee Reese appeared from within the woods on the first anniversary of his death, drifting out of evening shadows the way he once drifted under a windblown pop fly, passing from sunlight to shadow as he approached home. Though he moved with familiar grace, Pee Wee looked tired and old, ravaged by his long illness, but also elated to be back in the game. Without speaking he shared with me what he'd come to teach, that things would be all right, pain is nothing, stability is overrated, shattered sleep begets waking dreams. We can—we must—learn from our losses, Pee Wee reminded me, and illness is but a high pop fly that pulls us into shadow.

My Visitations were narrative, interactive, cohesive, and—unlike hallucinations—filled with factual information or detail I hadn't known previously. Although Eliot didn't speak, and remained beyond reach, he was right to remind me of voices singing out of empty cisterns and exhausted wells. It cost us $15,000, at thirty dollars a foot, to find the deep aquifer under our dry land. But the water *was* there.

I couldn't will them to happen, couldn't summon Visitors. If I could, there would have been Visits from Shakespeare or from Jules

Verne, master of the marvelous, whose work I treasure. From Maurice Ravel after aphasia silenced his music. From Flannery O'Connor or Vincent van Gogh, from Emily Dickinson. Hardy certainly would have appeared sooner. I'd have liked to see our landscape through Georgia O'Keeffe's eyes, and to have had time again with my father or brother. But my Visitations were spontaneous occurrences, surprises always. I came to think of them as an unfolding of the possible world.

⇌

I should also mention that a quarter century ago, at the age of forty-one, I contracted a virus that targeted my brain. All I'd done was take a flight from Portland to Washington, DC, but my doctors concluded that a virus carried on the plane's recirculating air supply was the likely pathogen. Human herpesvirus 6, they thought. Ubiquitous, but known for its neurovirulence among people whose immune systems can't manage it. Mine couldn't. The lesions made my brain look scattershot.

At first, the illness threatened to silence me. To dis-integrate me. Sometimes I would fail to find words at all, my mouth opening and closing, emitting a strangling squeak. Or I would say the same thing over and over. "How could it be August 8?" It took me a year to be able to read books with even minimal comprehension again, six years to be able to drive, fifteen years to walk without a cane, and I'm still learning to accommodate the ongoing persistent results of the lesions that have damaged my neurological functioning. Since 1988, I've been working to re-integrate myself.

I still say things like "Please fast the smooth" when I mean to say "Please pass the butter," or I tell Beverly that I've "numbed" the television rather than "muted" it. I use words that don't quite exist in the language, saying "the greenvers were swindy" when I meant "the evergreens were swaying in the wind." I carefully remove an empty cup from underneath the espresso maker's spout before turning the machine on and watch in confusion as the dark liquid cascades onto the countertop. We've lived in our current home for three years and I still can't remember if the window blinds should be slanted upward or downward to block the intense summer sun, though Beverly has told me I-don't-remember-how-many times.

To compose my work I learned to write fragments of thought on notepads or Post-its or index cards without worrying about errors and incorrect words, gather them in folders color-coded by topic or character or place, and go back over them later to see how they fit together. On longer projects, my desk becomes a kind of tidy but densely layered storyboard, one sheet for each idea or image or phrase, sheets shifting as related ones appear, a pathway toward discovering where I'm going. In a sense, my writing process embraces the gapped nature of my memory process, leaping across spaces that represent all I've lost and establishing fresh patterns within all that remains.

I don't stutter or stammer but I don't speak smoothly either, my sentences lurching and hitching along as I search for words, lose thoughts, forget questions, sense my ideas freefalling into the silences. I bump into walls; can't remember where I'm going or why; load laundry and soap into the washing machine and forget to turn it on; pick up a nearby stalk of celery rather than the ringing telephone and put it to my ear, surprised when no one responds. As I never did before getting sick, I cry over music, over sudden sunlight, acts of kindness and the ringtone that lets me know my daughter is calling and the discovery that my grocery store has begun to stock my favorite brand of organic nonfat Greek yogurt.

I came to understand that while I was different than I'd been before getting sick, that my cognitive powers had been measurably altered and my emotional responses had become less inhibited, there were noticeable benefits too. I was slower, more intuitive, open. I could sit still, could be content doing nothing in a place like our woods where there was so little to do. Sitting for hours under the trees one afternoon, I had a realization: this land was covered in second growth. Much of the hill's trees had been harvested many years ago and I was living within the density of what grew back. It was a good lesson in the slow process of returning from damage. I learned to live more fully in the moment because I could never be sure I'd remember that moment later. The moment might be all that I had.

I was off-kilter, yes, and for six months in the spring and summer of 2009 I had a sudden eruption of relentless vertigo that forced me back to my cane, and my sense of balance wasn't always stable even after I could walk caneless yet again. I had classical migraines for the first time. And I had Visitations. I had electrical disturbances in the brain.

But no doctor—and I've been seen by a vast array of medical specialists—found me to be psychologically ill. Not even the United States Social Security Administration, which for long-term disability purposes wanted very badly to find me mentally rather than neurologically disabled. They had me examined and tested, reexamined and retested by psychiatrists they hired themselves. They didn't send me to neurologists, but to shrinks for assessments of my mental status and to physical therapists for Functional Capacity Evaluations. I had to name in order all the presidents since Kennedy and count backward from one hundred by sevens, remember a list of words to recite twenty minutes later, stand on my left foot for as long as I could, fit a series of odd shapes into their proper slots on a form-board before time ran out. I had to lift weights, carry heavy boxes, push and pull loaded crates, climb stairs, play catch. I even had to crawl around the perimeter of a wrestling mat. They interviewed me over and over. One psychiatrist asked me to explain what was meant by the expression "People who live in glass houses should not throw stones." I knew that this sort of proverb relied on metaphor, which as a poet should be my great strength, and began to explain. Except that I couldn't. I must have talked for five minutes, in tortuous circles, spewing gobbledygook about stones breaking glass and people having things to hide, shaking my head, backtracking as I tried to elaborate. But it was beyond me, as all abstract thinking is beyond me. I lapsed into stunned silence. And in the end they determined I'm not schizophrenic, bipolar, psychotic, delusional, depressed. I don't have post-traumatic stress or dissociative identity disorder.

What I am is a man with post-viral encephalopathy, a man with brain lesions. Patchily rewired and glitchy. My IQ diminished by about 20 percent. It was as though I'd been geezered overnight. Fragmented. But there were compensatory gains and forays into strange territories. I know my perceptive abilities can sometimes be shaky, and that can be troubling. But I've learned to see that it can also be weirdly trustworthy, an opening into understanding hidden just an electric misfire away from me.

⊜

I bring all this up to get the he's-just-crazy card onto the table. I'm not, and yet when I heard Thomas Hardy speak to me, I felt a familiarity with the situation. It had been a while—there'd only been a few Visitations since our Yurt Era ended a half-dozen years ago, when Ezra Pound came to scold me for abandoning my home in the woods—but I felt right away that Hardy's contact was another Visitation. Real, vital, revelatory. But also intense and close-up, more intimate than previous Visitations had been, and more discomforting.

Sometimes Visitations coincided with a flaring of my illness, or occurred as part of the classic migraine aura, or when I'd taken pain medication or various herbal remedies or when I was overtired, stressed. But not always. Sometimes they simply happened, with no extenuating circumstances, as when Charles Dickens appeared out of the fog on the riverbank one Saturday in 2010. I was feeling fitter than I had since my vertigo had gone away the year before, taking a walk with Beverly, fresh from making love, holding her hand and hearing "Can't Take My Eyes Off You" by the Four Seasons in my head. Dickens emerged and was gone in an instant, but not before letting me know how fortunate I was to have what I had with my wife, and reminding me of all he'd risked for something similar.

As I said, I've had a few Visitations since getting sick. To be precise, I'd experienced twelve Visitations between 1993 and 2012. But none of the Visitors had come so close or physically touched me before. And none had returned to Visit again. Hardy's Visitation was different. And it felt incomplete. I knew in my soul he would be back.

2

Beverly rested the camera in her lap and gazed across South Street. Overhead, a red and yellow DORSET ART WEEK banner strung across the pedestrian walkway flapped in the wind. A man dressed in black from his fedora down to his trekking shoes stood at the NatWest Bank ATM and danced to the tune coming through his earphones.

"You saw something back there?" Beverly asked.

I nodded. "Felt and heard something too."

Though she never saw my Visitors, Beverly didn't doubt me. In part, that was because she'd had Visitations of her own, particularly during the Yurt Era. Most of hers were animal Visits.

In the spring months after she'd bought the twenty acres but before building the yurt, she'd spent a few weekend nights camped on the land, imagining potential home sites. She wanted to build near the center of the square-shaped property, and to clear as few trees as possible in the building process. The key was finding such a spot that was also near a water source where the well could be drilled and near the overgrown old logging road that would become the driveway. One night, as the problem of water was in her thoughts, Beverly drifted to sleep and woke in her down sleeping bag to hear great horned owls calling from nearby trees. When she sat up, there was a deer standing in a hoop of moonlight exactly where a dowser had told her the well should be dug. The deer looked at her and seemed to nod. A Visitation, all right, but it's too bad that deer failed to consider the effects of drought ten years in the future.

Besides, Beverly's years of dedicated spiritual practice had convinced her that such events were more than—and other than—hallucinatory, even if no one else could see them. There were dimensions to life that humans simply didn't understand. Hidden fields of force, like those warning wild animals to shelter before storms arrived or leading dowsers to water. She and I had lived so closely together for so long, it wasn't uncommon for us to experience shared thoughts, to finish—or even to start—each other's sentences, for the conventional barriers of Time and Space occasionally to be porous.

So when she said, "It was Hardy," I wasn't really surprised.

"Let's look at those pictures you took this morning in the museum," I said. She scrolled back through the camera's stored images, holding the monitor up so I could see it. "There."

Part of the Dorset County Museum's second floor is devoted to an exhibit called "A Writer's Dorset," complete with diaries, tributes, photographs, a startling reconstruction of Hardy's study that had been moved intact from Max Gate after his death. According to the museum brochure, its Hardy collection is the world's largest. Outside the room harboring his study, in the middle of the hallway, there's a life-size cardboard cutout of Hardy. His beard thick and dark, his hair trimmed, this Hardy is about half the age I am now. He's turned sideways in a desk chair with his elbow perched on its top rail, and he looks wary, sitting tight, as though certain that he's about to be torn from happy solitude. Which is exactly what I did, taking advantage of the early morning emptiness of the space, posing for two photographs with my arm draped around his shoulders.

As I studied the images in Beverly's camera, I was struck by the resemblance between Hardy's domed forehead and mine, and by our vigilant eyes, our similar size. I wondered if my act, that partial embrace in the museum hallway, had somehow summoned Hardy. At least let him know I was in Dorchester. Perhaps he'd summoned me, or rather any person with Hardy in mind, and my draped arm had signaled a readiness to rendezvous.

"He spoke to me."

"A Visitation," she said.

I nodded and repeated Hardy's words.

"'Something I missed' could mean almost anything."

"True, and I'm not sure I heard everything he said because at first I thought it was just the wind in my ear. But it sounded urgent. What mattered most to him. Say his writing or God or love—something he missed with those. Or about peace of mind, rest. A child? Maybe he missed having a child? Or acceptance from the highbrow critics? Travel beyond Europe?"

When I finally wound down, Beverly said, "You know, there's a whole other way to think about this. Is there something in you that prompted Hardy's Visit? Something connected to him or his writing. I don't know. Something you missed that only he can lead you to?"

She was right, of course. The Visitations sometimes seemed to answer questions I didn't know I had. Or made connections between fragments. "Like with T.S. Eliot," I said, "back in the woods when our well went dark. I mean dry. When our well went dry."

"His Visitation helped, didn't it? Gave you a way to face what we had to do. I still remember what you told me after he vanished: who better to remind us to look deep—something about tracing the history of our water all the way down to where the past became the future."

"When I saw him fading away, I was sure he said, 'There's a place where water always flows.'"

Beverly slipped her hand into the pocket of my vest and fished out one of the gluten-free snack bars we carried everywhere. We were silent for a minute or two as we ate. Then Beverly asked, "I mean, why did Thomas Hardy come to you? And is he answering a question for you?"

"Right. I have to find that out, too."

I'm hardly the first reader to have given himself over as a young man to Thomas Hardy's work. I came to him through his fiction, not his poetry. And I came to him through the influence of a teacher named Robert Russell, who was fond of saying "Thomas Hardy is not a good writer. But he is a great writer."

Russell was the first person I knew who had actually written a book. His memoir, *To Catch an Angel: Adventures in the World I Cannot See*, was published in 1962 and was selected by the Book-of-the-Month Club and included in the Reader's Digest Condensed Books series. My aunt Evelyn had read it and I remembered her talking during a family Seder about a courageous blind professor, making him fleetingly part of the family three years before I met him. The book was also reprinted in a sixty-cent paperback edition that I still own, tattered, emblazoned with testimonials about this "tough," "brave," "inspiring" man.

Russell was chair of the English Department and a specialist in Victorian literature at Franklin and Marshall College in Lancaster, Pennsylvania, when I arrived there as a freshman in the fall of 1965. Each year, he was provided with two student readers, and before classes began I was sent to meet him by the college's financial aid office. On the way, I stopped at the bookstore to leaf through *To Catch an Angel* and prepare myself to encounter a living writer. I remember the excitement of holding the book, seeing his photo, then closing my eyes and running my fingers around the edges to imagine how he felt when it first arrived.

Blinded at the age of five by a splintering croquet mallet, Russell had gone from being, as he wrote, "a citizen of the night," to being a graduate of Yale University and even a varsity wrestler there. Assertive, resourceful, resilient, he'd learned to navigate a world of obstacles, survived a wild bull attack, ridden a bicycle. After completing his doctoral work at Oxford University, he married Elizabeth Shaw, sister of the British actor Robert Shaw, who played the blond assassin in *From Russia with Love*. Russell had been teaching at Franklin and Marshall since 1955.

I was eighteen when we met, and had just spent the summer in bed recovering from a recurrence of mononucleosis, which I'd first contracted when I was eleven. Stuck there, I did enough concentrated reading, for the first time in my life, to learn that I needed eyeglasses. The reading had been haphazard and mostly provided by Aunt Evelyn because we didn't have books in our home. Well, that's not strictly true. As living room decor, never to be touched except when dusted, we had a matched set of a dozen red-covered books by French writers whose surnames my mother loved to declaim, Zola, Balzac, Flaubert, Maupassant, Stendhal. But focused boyhood reading—the novels of adventure and escape and survival, the stories of friendship and its power, of exploration and discovery—was something I missed. No Robinson Crusoe or Captain Nemo or Sherlock Holmes, no Robert Louis Stevenson or H. G. Wells or Jack London. I have no recollection of being in a bookstore as a child. My mother left school after the ninth grade and my father, a poultry butcher, worked fourteen-hour days six days a week. I have no recollection of being read to or of hearing a conversation in my family about literature. What I read was comic books, the backs of baseball cards, the occasional Hardy Boys book passed along by a friend.

But the summer I turned eighteen, there was a pile of books on the chair beside my sickbed. I read popular novels that my aunt read, two weeks after she finished them. Arthur Hailey's *Hotel*, Bel Kaufman's *Up the Down Staircase*, James Michener's *The Source*. And I read Harvey Cox's *The Secular City* and B. F. Skinner's *Walden Two*, both assigned by Franklin and Marshall for freshmen orientation week. I could feel myself filling with language, ideas, scenes, like a parched man finally reaching water.

As of September 1965, when I arrived at college, the only classics I'd read were those required in high school, *Silas Marner*, *Great Expectations*, *The Return of the Native*, *Romeo and Juliet*. Unformed, with no idea what I wanted to be or do or study, just yearning to get away and grow, I didn't even know enough to know how little I knew.

Still weak, anxious to impress Russell, barely balanced between awe and fear, I found him, covered in pipe ash, rocking back in his office chair. He instructed me to sit beside his desk, handed over a sheet of paper, and said, "Read this letter to me, would you?"

He was the best listener I'd ever been around. He seemed to listen with his entire head, eyebrows aquiver, forehead wrinkling and straightening, the plane of his skull undergoing minute adjustments as I spoke.

His hands were clasped and feet crossed as though shutting down everything that wasn't part of the hearing mechanism. Even his hair, stuck out like antennae, seemed part of the process.

A few minutes later, I was hired as his reader, a job I held through the next four years. Squeezed into a side chair between his desk and door, I read student papers aloud to him, pausing so he could type comments. I read personal correspondence and departmental memos, magazine and newspaper articles, proofs of his forthcoming novel, *An Act of Loving.* Pacing my words to match his strokes, I read passages from poems or essays as he typed them in braille. After a few months, in those days before audio books were widely available, he occasionally asked me to record novels or extended selections of poetry onto tape for him. Using a vacant storage room near his office as my studio, and working with his enormous reel-to-reel machine, I read works of literature in a way few young, would-be authors get to do, experiencing stories or poems in the old way, orally, passing them along as a conduit between author and audience, giving them voice.

I recorded all the selections of Victorian writers included in *The Norton Anthology of English Literature: Major Authors Editions*: 40 pages of Carlyle, 100 pages of Tennyson, 74 pages of Browning, 104 pages of Arnold, and 16 pages of Hardy. I recorded a half-dozen novels, too, but can only remember William Faulkner's *The Sound and the Fury* and Hermann Hesse's *Steppenwolf,* probably because reading them aloud drove me nuts.

Russell himself, and what Russell required me to do as a reader, had exposed the great possibilities for human contact within the acts of writing and reading. In *To Catch an Angel,* he'd written about the moment when literature had first moved him deeply. He was eighteen, a college freshman, still recovering from the shock of his father's sudden death, when a literature teacher assigned "The Wife of Usher's Well." This Scottish ballad deals with the death at sea of a woman's three sons who, in answer to her wish, miraculously return home for one night. When they must leave in the morning, one of the brothers says farewell to the scullery maid as well as to the mother, and Russell's teacher asked the class why. To his surprise, Russell found himself answering the question. He understood that the servant "symbolized all the comfort and pleasure and security that home had meant" for the brother. He understood, too, "the longing for the familiar pattern of life at home," and connected that longing with what had happened in his own life when his father died. "I understood then that this ballad was about people, real people, people who lived and felt as I did," and "for the first time, I was deeply moved by a poem."

Something similar happened to me in my storage room studio, alone with the work Russell assigned. Great writing, I saw, could stop time and thereby make time come to life, transporting the reader, as it must have transported the writer, into another dimension. It could break down the barriers between writer, reader, and characters. Speak for and through them all. I became avid for reading, for literature and the discussion of literature. I didn't know how to speak about it yet, had no voice for what I was feeling, but knew I was in the right place to learn how.

I spent so much time in the English Department offices, being in close contact with Russell daily, that it wasn't surprising I became an English major. When I took Major British Writers or Intro to Drama from him while also working for him, we were sometimes together six hours a day. When I played my first game for the college's freshman base-ball team, and slid into third base for a lead-off triple, I was astonished to find Russell sitting on a small hill in foul territory cheering me on. It was a powerful relationship for me, and he became the closest thing to a father I'd had since my father, like Russell's, had suddenly died.

I was fourteen when my father and mother had gone to a resort in upstate New York for the weekend. He'd been active and happy there, horseback riding, swimming, playing pinochle, glad to have a Saturday away from his working life. Sunday, after a few minutes under the pool-side sunlamp, he wanted a quick cool-off before heading upstairs to change for dinner. So he dove into the water, where he had a heart attack and drowned.

I believed for years that if I'd been there I could have saved him. Would have seen him flailing in the deep end and known he was in trouble. Or I could have changed the entire scenario by asking him to play catch with me, pinball. We could learn croquet. I believed I would not have let him die.

Obsessed with my father's death, I was unable to stop thinking about the last moments he'd been alive and what might have been going through his mind. Had he thought about me? We were both going about our business unaware that the seconds were ticking down. I replayed in my mind the last time I'd seen him alive, his back to me as he walked through the door with luggage in his hands, the smell of his Havana cigar lingering in the air. Did he kiss me? Did I remember the rough feel of his whiskers or the scent of Old Spice?

Under Russell's influence, I began trying to write poems and read them to him. How kind he was to listen, and to encourage, when the poems were so awful. So inauthentic, with no notion of how to speak about what I felt. Instead of commenting about the poems, he asked me questions.

"What did your father do for a living?"

"He owned a live poultry market and killed chickens all day."

"Did you ever see him do that?

"A few times. The chickens screamed whenever he came near their coops. He'd grab one, draw his super-sharp knife from someplace inside his apron, and slit the chicken's neck. It made me cry and he stopped letting me come to the market."

"What did he look like?"

"People say he looked like me. Or I guess they say I look like him."

"Well, that's fine, that's very evocative, but it doesn't tell a blind man much. What did he look like?"

"Short, maybe five-three. Bald, blocky. His nose was flat from when a chicken coop fell on him and his fingers were all gnarled and nicked. He sometimes had blood or feathers still stuck to his neck when he got home. He smelled."

"Like what?"

"Meat." I thought for a moment and added, "Cigars. He smoked big fat ones."

"What did you talk about together?"

I'd never thought about that, could hardly remember the sound of my father's voice anymore. "We didn't talk much, Dr. Russell. He was already gone to his market when I woke up in the morning and he got home late, seven o'clock. Mostly what he wanted from me then was silence. I saw him on Sundays. Sometimes we all went to visit his widowed mother. Sometimes we went to the cemetery where his father was buried. We talked about who would get buried where in the family plot."

I remember the sound of Russell breathing as he processed my answer, the room so still around us. "That day when he died," he asked, "how did you get the news?"

"Someone called." When Russell didn't say anything, I understood what his silence meant. "His friend Harry." Which startled me to remember because my father's name was also Harry and their voices were similar.

"What were you doing when the call came?"

"I was in my room playing a game I'd invented." More silence. "Dice baseball. I used to keep endless statistics in a notebook." Then I found myself unable to speak. Russell waited. "Oh. I remember once my father got so angry that he tore my notebook apart. A year's worth of statistics."

"Go on, there's more, isn't there?"

"Yes. The next night. He didn't exactly apologize—not with words, anyway—but when he came home from the market he walked past my bedroom and flipped a pack of baseball cards onto my bed. He'd never done anything like that before. A few seconds later he walked by in the other direction and flipped another pack. He did that five times without saying anything."

"These are the things you need to be writing in your poems, Floyd. You loved your father and you miss him, of course you do. But simply saying those words won't let others feel what's really in your heart. *Your* heart. The poem doesn't sound like you, it sounds like everyone. To love someone is to speak your heart to them."

"Even if you don't use words."

"Like your father? Well, yes. But in a poem or a story you do need words."

As my junior year was ending, Russell said that, during the summer, I should think about a topic for my senior honors thesis. He'd be happy to supervise me. I wanted to work with him as well, though that narrowed my options primarily to Victorian writers. So in the fall of 1968, having done little more about the matter than glance through an anthology of Victorian literature, I sat in his office just before classes began and said what I thought he wanted to hear: "Browning," thinking, Oh no, not ten months of Browning! Russell's brows twitched, a language I now knew how to read, so I said, "Or maybe Arnold." He rocked back and remained silent. "Not Tennyson," I added.

"How about Thomas Hardy?"

I'd recorded those 16 pages of Hardy's gloomy poems, and seen the 1,002-page volume of *Collected Poems* in the bookstore. "You mean all the poetry?"

"I was thinking of the novels. I have a feeling for Hardy, and I think you might too."

I recalled tolerating *The Return of the Native* in high school, and sort of liking *The Mayor of Casterbridge* when I'd read it for extra credit. But that was four years ago, and I didn't remember much about either book except they both had a bunch of explosive, angry characters storming around the Dorset countryside. I'd seen the film of *Far from the Madding Crowd* the previous fall, though, and Julie Christie was a gorgeous Bathsheba. Okay, since I already knew three Hardy novels, and had heard of two more (*Tess of the D'Urbervilles* and *Jude the Obscure*) in my introduction to Hardy's poetry, I had a good head start on the work. After all, how many novels could Hardy have written?

We agreed on Hardy. "Draw up a schedule," he said. "Let's do each novel in sequence, one every two weeks, all right?"

He took my inhalation as agreement.

"Why don't we use the first week for you to give me a summary of the plot and characters. Second week to go over your commentary."

I remember that day very clearly. I walked from the English Department office across campus to the library in a Pennsylvania version of British mist. But passing the brick buildings of the campus core made me feel the familiar sense of being exactly where I belonged, in a setting I loved, doing what I loved. Nothing better than starting a new term, getting new books, plunging into new material. As a twenty-one-year-old who imagined himself a budding writer, I was getting a chance to immerse myself in the work of a master, someone who wrote both poetry and prose, as I hoped to do. My creative future felt very close.

Just a few minutes after clacking across the library's marble floor I'd found the shocking answer to my question. Thomas Hardy had written fourteen novels. With a full load of classes, daily work as Russell's reader, acting in the college theater, and trying to write poetry, it was going to be a busy senior year.

⇶

After completing my senior thesis, I kept copies of Hardy's novels with me as I moved from one house and one state to another, sixteen moves in all, Hardy always hauled along, even when I had to get rid of so many books in order to share Beverly's yurt in the woods. Not just hauled along, but reread. A touchstone for me, across time and place.

Also, that first year after I got sick, a source of hope. For months during the most acute phase of my illness—winter and early spring of 1989—I could read nothing more complicated than *People* magazine or *TV Guide*. Those would take a week to complete and I could recall little of what I read. In July, I managed to finish a thriller, forgetting details and names as I went along but carried forward on a scene-by-scene narrative current. I felt as surprised and stupefied by its plot developments as the story's unsuspecting characters. Spending all day in bed or in my recliner, I began using a yellow highlighter to help reinforce the retention of detail, and read Elmore Leonard, Ross Thomas, Sue Grafton, going over sentences again and again, trying to keep details clear, voices distinct and present. At the end of autumn, fully a year after that plane trip to Washington, DC, I picked up Thomas Hardy's last novel, the dark impassioned, fate-harrowed *Jude the Obscure*. Being able to read it, to really read again, following the story and characters with all their twists and turns, gave me my first real sense of hope that I would be able to come back. Makes me laugh to think about that now, about deriving hope from the most hopeless novel written by one of the most hope-deprived novelists in literary history. But finishing *Jude the Obscure* not only let me feel that I was getting back some minimal capacity to focus and think and hold things in mind, it let me feel that I could connect with who I'd been before getting sick. That I would find my way back to coherence in my life. Hardy, once again, at the center for me.

It wasn't just Hardy's novels themselves that mattered. Increasingly, grateful for what felt like rescue, I'd become interested in his life too. Over the next twenty-three years I'd read eight Hardy biographies, including the self-ghostwritten one. I'm not saying I remembered all the details, but I felt that by the time we reached Dorset I had a strong sense of him.

≑

So okay, I'm a sixty-four-year-old man who's been reading Hardy for 70 percent of his life, and who finally made the trip to Hardy country. I'm brain damaged and subject to Visitations, engaged in an ongoing struggle to integrate what has been shattered by neurological damage. I'm unabashedly in love with my wife of twenty years. I write poems and memoirs and fiction. All of that still doesn't give me a full enough answer to Beverly's question about why Hardy came to me. But I'm on the case.

We began walking back to the car park. Higher Bockhampton, where Hardy was born and raised, was only about three miles away, but I found myself wondering, idiotically, whether he could reach me there if he wanted to. Maybe I should hang around Dorchester for a while, just in case. I stopped walking and looked around. We were back to High Street, in front of the Dorset County Museum again. Beverly was a few steps ahead, consulting her map as she walked.

No, of course Hardy could reach me. We'd had contact and I felt that he knew where I was. The next move would be his to make. After all, he was at home everywhere around here, and accustomed to walking it all as freely as the butterflies in the cornfields flying straight down High Street without any apparent consciousness that they were traversing strange latitudes.

As I watched Beverly, her long legs and strong back, her clear sense of where she was in space and where she was heading, it occurred to me that it could be us together—me and Beverly—that sparked the Visitation from Hardy.

One thing his work and his life made clear was how terribly he struggled with love. I remembered reading about his thwarted, often overwhelming early passions; a long, fraught, anguishing first marriage shadowed by his feeble attempts at affairs, his compulsion to withdraw, conflict over matters of class, childlessness, and guilt-ridden grief after his wife died; a late-life marriage to a woman forty years his junior who had served him as a kind of secretary. Hardy seemed to believe love could happen, but not that it could last.

And here he was now, eighty-four years after his death, so troubled over something missed that he haunted the landscape perhaps in hopes of finding it still. Maybe what he missed was some idea of love that went beyond the love he knew or could imagine for his characters, a love that would endure. Or maybe what he missed was writing about it in a way that satisfied him. Did he stop before he got there? Could it be that the scholars and aficionados all had it wrong, and there was—as rumored—a lost true love that served to torment Hardy throughout the rest of his life? Something he grasped but couldn't or wouldn't hold onto. Could it be that what he missed was the secret to keeping love alive? Or hope or faith?

I felt that Hardy was handing me a gift, one that I could only understand by writing about it. I caught up to Beverly, and told her what I'd been thinking. Then I said, "This Visitation from Hardy feels like something to do with a book."

She nodded because she already knew that. "What kind?"

All I could do at that point was shrug. Beverly didn't necessarily expect an answer. She was helping me think. "When Hardy vanished, it was like he'd slipped back between pages of a book. For a moment, I felt he was still around. The story was in progress, the book was in my hands, there just weren't any words written in it yet. I have to stay with that feeling." We'd almost reached the car park. "I have to find out what that book is."

"Investigative journalism with phantoms as sources."

"And subjects."

3

The drive from downtown Dorchester to Higher Bockhampton took less than ten minutes. At Cuckoo Lane, a name straight out of Hardy's novel *Under the Greenwood Tree*, we looped back over the highway and found the narrow road to his long low cottage with a hipped roof of thatch. The cottage was a National Trust site now, and no longer quite the lonely and silent spot between woodland and heathland.

Still, I felt nervous, almost shy at the thought of being there, where a doctor in 1840, believing him dead, had thrown aside the newborn child. On the first evening in June, Jemima Hand Hardy had gone into labor attended by Lizzie Downton, a midwife who lived in one of the seven homes along this isolated lane beside the heath. Downstairs, Jemima's husband of five months and her mother-in-law spent the night in their hard chairs or stepping outside for the cool spring air as the screams grew more desperate. When the sun rose on June 2, flooding the bedroom where Jemima lay exhausted, the doctor was finally summoned. "You should have sent for me sooner," he said, glancing at the limp Hardy and tossing him into a nearby basket. "I must try to save the mother." Hardy junkies know what happened next, and can recite Lizzie's words as she rescued the frail and fragile thing: "Dead! Stop a minute: he's alive enough, sure!"

So Hardy was delicate from the get-go. Sickly. Came to life all tangled up with death, straddling the border, by birth a citizen of both realms. As we all are, of course, but Hardy more intensely so, his work saturated in doom, haunted by death, the last link in the chain of faith that rules his characters. He arrived on the verge of abandonment, of rejection, and from the first breath could never feel sure he was loved enough or mattered enough to keep. Grown up, he was sensitive to the least slights, defensive, a connoisseur of wounds and humiliations, slow to heal, a hoarder of grudges, scarred by the early absence of love's certainty.

The drama of his birth set the tone for his time at home. He called Higher Bockhampton quaint, passed it off as a quiet and isolated little settlement or snug homestead of his child-time, the treasured relic of bygone days. But it held drama aplenty for the young Hardy, drama he never ceased to draw upon in his fiction and poetry.

For every story like the one about an infant Hardy found asleep in his cradle with a large snake curled upon his breast, there's a counter-balancing story like the one about him lying on his back watching sun-rays stream through the straw hat he'd placed over his face, leading him to conclude that he did not wish to grow up. And he didn't grow up, or not at the usual pace. Hardy himself said his immaturity was greater than is common for his years. He said he was a child till he was sixteen, a youth till he was twenty-five, and a young man till he was nearly fifty. He lived with his parents and three younger siblings in the secluded, crowded seven-roomed rambling house of his childhood—except for a five-year interlude in London during his midtwenties—until marrying at the age of thirty-four.

Shy and aloof, he was also ecstatic of temperament and wildly sensi-tive to music. When his father played the violin, little Tommy—as he called himself—would stand alone in the middle of the smoky room and dance to the tunes while weeping at their lyrics. He learned to fiddle young and would play with such frenzied zeal that he'd eventually collapse by the hearth. Later, he traveled with his father and uncle to play at harvest suppers, wishing the songs would never end, his soul lifted beyond time or place, his rare smile real as a window.

He learned to read almost before he learned to walk, learned to laugh without making a sound, learned to know a day was over by watching sundown set his home's red staircase walls ablaze. He thought he was useless, invisible though everyone seemed to see whatever he did.

His parents fought; his mother advised him never to wed, to live instead with his sister Mary. I recall the poignant picture of a round-faced, stiff-backed, unsmiling, self-conscious Hardy at sixteen, crafted sprig of moustache barely visible over his grim lip, hair no more successfully tamed than the cravat blossoming from his skewed collar, large zit on his brow, posing with a massive hat clutched under his right arm as he tries to appear twenty-five rather than twelve. The boy who didn't want to grow up wanted to be a grown-up.

⁂

A quarter-mile shy of the Hardy cottage, vehicle traffic was directed to a turnoff for the Thorncombe Wood parking lot. It was nearly empty. We got out of the car and looked around as we stretched. Directly across the pitted access road stood the Greenwood Grange Farm Cottages, a sprawling complex of brick, stone, and slate barns and outbuildings converted into luxury holiday accommodations. My first thought was that if we'd stayed there, Hardy could have sat down with us for dinner last night, in private, in a location where he'd feel comfortably close to home, a deluxe place named after his lovely second novel composed just a few hundred yards away, and maybe we could have gotten our business—whatever it might be—done right then.

"So what is it you believe you missed, Tom?"

Clearly, such a meeting wasn't part of the plan. Nor was Greenwood Grange within our budget. Besides, Beverly and I were happy with our B&B near Lulworth Cove, and Hardy knew his way around that area too.

We entered the woodland where a fingerpost pointed us toward Hardy's cottage. The wide trail rolled through sun-flecked oak, sweet chestnut, beech, a few birch and holly, and across a warm clearing. Downed, mossy limbs and thick scrub marked the edges.

"Hear that?" Beverly said. "That's a song thrush. Wait, over there. Hear the woodpecker?"

She took photos as we walked, capturing the trail's gentle rise and fall, the feeling of apparent isolation mingled with lush hidden life. We passed a small wooden waymarker for Hardy's beloved Rushy Pond, where he'd walked with his parents on Sunday mornings and where he came by himself to stare at images in the wind-stirred surface.

I knew we were moving along the margins of a place to which Hardy had given vivid fictional life—majestic, bleak Egdon Heath, ancient moorland, wild and unwelcoming, thorny and somber, a near relation of night, as Hardy described it—and thought I should utter some incantation that would breach whatever dimension separated us. Reach out to him. But I realized he was, in essence, all around me. I was so conscious of his presence in this Hardy heartland that I needed to focus simply on that. I thought I could even hear the spectral sound of something swishing through the underbrush.

Then it was easy to see him passing through these woods as a teenager, walking to visit his cousins in Puddletown, who were also his first loves. Their home, Sparks Corner, was only a couple of miles away, at the end of Puddletown Forest, a cheerful place with the river right in front. But he wasn't sure how welcome he'd be after the Christmas Mummers' rehearsal, when he'd tried to kiss and caress his cousin Rebecca as she sat sewing by the fire. It had been a night of music and drinking, Hardy was stirred, feeling almost bewitched. Rebecca and her younger sister Martha looked so full of life, happy. Song was everywhere. He was suddenly overwhelmed, didn't know what to do with his fervor, and hurled himself at Rebecca. She was eleven years older, and so shocked at his sudden advances that at first she didn't resist. So he'd instinctively pushed her back and started to climb up on the narrow seat with her before she gathered herself enough to throw him aside (another instance of being thrown aside!). His aunt Mary chased Hardy from the house and told him not to come back. He was hoping that enough time had elapsed with the passing of winter and spring. He knew he had no chance with Rebecca, of course, but by now maybe Martha would welcome his attention. He'd always thought she was beautiful, her features like the best of his mother's but full of warmth and mirth. She was older than Hardy too, but only by six years, and seemed so affectionate toward him. Maybe he would marry her someday. Those winter and spring months had been a crazed period for Hardy, fired by unfamiliar surges of desire, particularly for girls he hardly knew. He said he fell madly in love with one in Dorchester, a total stranger who passed by on horseback and smiled at him; said he admired a pink and plump damsel in the Sunday School class he taught, lost his heart for a few days to another who'd come to Dorset from Windsor, was drawn to a fourth who won Hardy's boyish admiration because of her beautiful bay red hair, formed an attachment to a farmer's daughter named Louisa that went deeper. He longed to speak with her, but could only manage a murmured "Good evening" that was met with silence. Looking back in old age, Hardy wondered if his late development afforded a clue to his character and action. Maybe, I thought, that's a clue to what Hardy feels he missed, the natural growth in which his mind and body, nature and behavior, cohered.

⇌

The trail curled and sloped down behind Hardy's cottage. From that perspective, the thatch roof looked tinny in the spring sunlight and the cob walls gleamed. Boughs of old beeches drooped overhead and brambles butted through a wooden fence. We saw some well-worn brick facing, a couple of small windows—one of them barred—and I was struck by the starkness. Weekly workers employed by Hardy's father would come back there to receive wages through the window.

A few yards farther, the trail reached a crossroads. We stopped to read the inscription on a ten-foot-high granite monument, which said it had been erected there in Hardy's memory by a few of his American admirers in 1931.

"Nice laurel wreaths," Beverly said, touching the brass decoration on the stone's rough-hewn face.

Then we walked around the building into a profusion of plants and shrubs, the old apple trees and honeysuckle, the thick box and laurestinus bushes Hardy had written about. A wooden wheelbarrow rested just beyond the off-center front door, with a small table standing beyond that, covered in a flowery cloth and set up for tea.

Before entering the cottage, we walked away from it, heading west along the manicured pathways to get some distance and see its face afresh. Last night, preparing for this visit, I'd read Beverly the early passage from *Under the Greenwood Tree* in which a group of local musicians approaches the cottage from where we now stood and sees these three dormer windows breaking up into the eaves, a chimney standing in the middle of the ridge and another at each end. Now we were back within the spell of a Hardy novel, letting ourselves dwell in its rare happy, rustic opening mood, real life and fictional life merging again.

The cottage door opened and a man wearing a bright-red T-shirt stood filling the space. Among all the browns and greens and whites, he was the brightest thing around, the center that irresistibly drew my eye. He positioned himself on the porch just to the left of the door, directly beneath the upstairs middle window—the room where Hardy had been born—and leaned back against the wall. He was enjoying the sun, which gleamed off his bald skull. He was taking a break, doing no harm. But it distracted me to see him there, or rather to be unable not to see him there. I thought if he'd worn beige or gray I'd have felt better.

What I couldn't do was incorporate his presence into the vista. Something about him simply couldn't be absorbed. As we started to approach the cottage, I noticed that the closer we got, the smaller he became. It made no sense, but I plainly saw his long head contract, his florid shirt shrink. Beverly stopped to take photos of the cottage and grounds, which gave me time to back up and determine what would happen to the man. He grew larger again. Even for me, this was weird.

I looked up at the smoke drifting out of the chimney. A June fire was necessary to help keep the earthy walls dry, but it seemed like a Hollywood effect: warmth in the aged inglenook, smell of ash, wispy vapor heading toward the heavens. Then I looked back at the man in red and noticed his resemblance to a photograph of Thomas Hardy II, the novelist's hardworking hard-playing father. Thomas and Tommy made cider together using apples from those trees right there, the son often lost in the father's shadow. They walked onto the heath behind the house and took turns gazing at the landscape through a brass telescope. He was, like his son, most at home all over here, so it made sense that he'd linger too.

From where I stood, the man's face was now in a bit of haze, but I thought I could see the familiar puffy white beard along his jaw and the wings of hair at his hat-line. The way he looked at sixty-six, in the photo appearing in every biography of his son. That thin, wide line, like the first draft of a mouth. The strength in his body even then, and steady blue eyes that showed he was seldom surprised by anything he saw, a man who knew what he knew. This was the Thomas Hardy who was comfortable around women, who drew them to himself naturally. Who married the woman he'd gotten pregnant and brought her home to live in the cottage where his mother also lived.

Was he here now, I wondered, to offer me welcome or discouragement? He was known as a courteous, charming man, but a grave, forbidding blankness marked this figure's demeanor. I wasn't going to get close enough to clarify anything, since I could only see him from afar. Which led me to realize he intended to show me something about the love his son had missed. Stand back, stand still, and watch.

At that moment, the man's image became brilliantly clear, its features snapping into focus. I was in the right spot to see that this was the younger Thomas Hardy after all, the writer at almost thirty, recognizably himself with the full dark beard and evasive gaze. But there was a half smile, an amusement in his expression that I don't remember seeing in photos. The red draped over his chest was, I saw, not a shirt at all. It was a bundle, perhaps an infant wrapped in a blanket, something like a small head now visible at Hardy's shoulder. I thought I heard the softest intimation of song.

The thought of Hardy tenderly holding a child, perhaps a child of his own, carried a wallop of sadness. Biographers have long made the point that the failure to have children was the most tragic thing about his life. Something he always regretted. I remember reading that Hardy had a gift for connecting with other people's children—provided they were quiet and well behaved—and loved visiting their families, affectionate, never forgetting to say goodnight. Learning that a former servant was pregnant, Hardy wrote in his notebook, "Yet never a sign of one is there for us."

Beverly walked up beside me and said, "I wish that bald-headed guy in the red shirt would move away. Can't get a good shot of the front door."

Then we both heard the sound of a violin. It was coming from inside the cottage, a few random notes that soon coalesced into a reel.

✥

In her forties, early in our life together, Beverly bought a used violin, some instruction books and sheet music, took a few lessons, and began to play. Soon she was devoting a couple hours a day to it. Sound travels oddly in a round house, swirling and amplifying, seeming to come from everywhere at once, and I loved to sit downstairs in the room where I wrote, listening to her practice upstairs. She'd do her scales, work on classical passages, Chopin and Bach, on Irish folk tunes and Beatles ballads, Cole Porter, Gershwin.

I remember her playing "Turkey in the Straw" late one day as summer light softened toward dusk. It was the peak of a three-week heat wave, the yurt sweltering because its large windows and skylight were designed to collect heat, and as usual at such times we'd stripped down as the day progressed. Soon I heard her feet begin shuffling of their own accord, keeping the beat, and I imagined the room filling with music that circled her gleaming figure before spiraling down to find and embrace me where I sat. It was purely sensual, a caress of melody, and it was also sharply sexual. I knew and loved the way her hands moved. Her body, her lips as the song progressed. Outside, as though summoned by her tune, the wind picked up, whirling around the lilies blooming in our yard, making the cherry and oak leaves sway, shadows dance. All I could see and feel seemed caught up in her playing, loosed by it, and I began to sing of sugar in the gourd and honey in the horn. I'd never been so happy since the day I was born.

34

At Christmas, Beverly participated in a violin recital at a retirement home in McMinnville, a dozen miles north of us. Her group prepared to play the "Christmas Hornpipe" and "Snowflake Reel," and I remember being mesmerized as I watched her perform, seeing her concentration as she gave herself over to the group. It was both individual—I'd seen how hard she'd worked to get this reel right and to perfect her solos—and communal, the essence of that holiday's spirit. Just the sort of musical gathering that Hardy and his family loved to be part of. I was deeply touched by witnessing it.

Once the music came into our life, it began to spread. Beverly soon bought a flute and taught herself to play. As she practiced its higher notes, our cats would flee through the flap door and head for the woods. We added a soprano recorder and then, since she loved Celtic music, a pennywhistle too. Since she'd had piano lessons as a child, we got an electronic piano. She'd plug in headphones so her practices would be silent, but I loved to hear the soft clacking of her keys, the clicks of the sustain pedal, her breath and occasional vocalizing of random notes. She shifted her weight and from behind I saw what seemed to be her body's own pure harmony as she moved, a kind of lyricism of muscle and skin, soul given expression. After we left the country for the city, she taught herself the guitar—classical, then blues—and the ukulele, and I never tire of listening and watching her explore the music in herself.

Beverly is a beautiful woman. Lean, long, with strong wide shoulders, a former swimming champion who specialized in the butterfly stroke. To see her in water is to see her fully at ease, but she has a radiant elegance of movement on land too. Blonde and fair, not given to makeup or artificiality, she never pretends to be other than she is. And she has dozens of different laughs, each bringing its own unique light to her hazel eyes. A quiet, too, which is what I saw as we entered Hardy's cottage to the reel's even beats.

4

The space inside seemed impossibly small. Even at five foot four I felt the need to hunch my shoulders as I gazed around the ground floor. Smoke and murk from the fireplace intensified the sense of closeness, as did the looming, dark, bisecting ceiling beam. Hardy's parents and siblings—the six of them, plus his grandmother until she died when Hardy was sixteen—lived in this little area for all those years? They had guests, cooked, dined, played music, danced, conducted business? And Hardy worked—wrote four novels—perched on the window seat in a cramped, slant-roofed room upstairs that he shared with his kid brother, Henry?

I could easily imagine Hardy's mother with her fiercely demanding, censorious personality, overwhelming everyone and everything in these tight quarters. That's what my mother had done in our tiny Brooklyn apartment. She'd screamed and stomped, her voice ever present in both bedrooms and the living room and kitchen, inescapable. She saw me wherever I was, or could detect whatever I'd done from a quick scan of the evidence, appearing out of nowhere all of a sudden. Once when I was around five she caught me playing with two toys at once, a small tank and a large fort.

"How dare you!" she shouted from the doorway of my room. "I've told you to put away one toy before you take out another."

"But they go together."

"Don't you backtalk me." She marched over, picked up the two toys, and threw them in my red wooden toy chest. Then she grabbed me and threw me in there too. "In you go." She slammed the lid and sat on it.

I lay on my side in the darkness, sharp edges from the toys digging into my hip and ribs, and knew exactly what I had to do: keep silent, don't cry, breathe small, wait.

"What happened?" At first I didn't know who'd spoken. I wanted to say "Ssshhhhhh," so my mother wouldn't get angrier and keep me in there longer. My heartbeat was so accelerated I could barely catch my breath. I was sweating, my skin prickly. But then Beverly touched me and I was back beside her.

"Cramped space," I whispered, panting, and she knew what I meant. "I'm okay." For a moment there, it was like I'd been trapped in some kind of neural storm, a waking night terror.

Beverly and I stood just inside the front door of Hardy's cottage, looking into the living room where a young woman sat in an armless bentwood chair. With Beverly's hand in mine, I could feel myself relax into the present moment. Paperback editions of Hardy's novels were stacked on the lace-covered table beside her. She had a bonnet on her short dark hair, and topaz stones studded her earlobes. Over jeans and polo she wore an old-fashioned white smock. Her eyes behind granny glasses roamed the room as she fiddled, seeing but not seeing. Beverly and I remained still while the reel spun out.

After a brief silence in which I couldn't decide whether it would be proper to applaud, Beverly said, "That was lovely. It was 'The Fairy Dance,' wasn't it?"

The young woman smiled and nodded. "Thank you. Welcome to Thomas Hardy's birthplace."

I wasn't sure exactly what I wanted to say next. Are you real? I was glad Beverly had seen and heard her.

What I managed to utter was "Do you, I mean who, but, well."

"I work for the National Trust, and I actually live here about half the year." She placed the violin on the table beside Hardy's novels, and stood. "My name's Katie." We shook hands. "Do you have any questions or would you just like to walk around by yourselves?"

Have you seen him lately? Because I happen to know he's out and about.

"You said you live here?" I asked.

"I do. I like it. They need somebody to take care of the buildings and property. And greet visitors, of course." Katie took a step toward the fireplace and spread her arms, pointing to both the front and back walls. She was shifting into a prepared speech, but it sounded urgent too. "Very little has altered since Hardy's time. We say the cottage is alive and after being here awhile you can see it really is. I mean, it's made out of local mud and chalk and sand and straw and even tree branches, it breathes and weeps, and the walls just turn to goo if you don't heat them up every day."

I think it was the word *alive* that caught me. I glanced at Beverly and found her already looking at me. Katie was still pointing at the walls but was looking down at the stone floors.

"Are you from the area?" I asked her, "or was there some other reason you wanted to be here instead of a different National Trust property?"

"Both." She smiled. "I was born and raised in London but my family's from Dorset. Mostly Dorchester and Chettle, but through the whole Frome valley too." She paused, reached out to adjust the position of the violin. I found myself thinking, Go on, please go on. But I knew I had to wait in silence as she decided whether to say more. Eyes still on the violin, she said, "My full name is Katie Pole Crosbie."

Oh. I repeated it to myself and thought, Maybe this is a test. There would be no further explanation of why she wanted to be here unless I understood how her full name was relevant. That I knew what it signified, and didn't simply offer our names in return.

"Pole." I took a slow breath. "As in Cassie Pole?"

"Cousin on my father's side, five generations back." As Katie spoke, I felt a presence brush up against my side. Beverly, I realized after a jolting heartbeat.

"Who was Cassie Pole?" she asked.

Katie turned to us, her voice now much softer. "She was a ladies' maid, a butler's daughter, and, well, she was also Thomas Hardy's sweetheart for a good while. He called her 'one I had rated rare' in a poem he wrote after she died. Said she was someone he 'loved as a lass.' In my family, they always said he'd bought her a ring. The same ring he eventually gave to his wife, Emma. But his family disapproved of him marrying Cassie because she was a servant, and he jilted her."

"Then," I said, "he showed up for dinner at the rector's house, where the butler happened to be Cassie Pole's father. It was one of those notorious only-in-Thomas-Hardy's-world moments of coincidence. The butler having to wait upon a stonemason's son who'd spurned his sweet daughter now that he was a famous writer."

Katie shrugged. "There are quite a few families around Dorset with stories like ours. I've heard of at least three who also claim they received the same ring. Hardy fell in love a lot."

"And apparently out a lot too," Beverly said. "Quickly."

"It's not the first thing people think of when they think of Thomas Hardy as a man. But the odd thing is, I feel glad to be here. You know, I think he really loved Cassie for a time, loved her intensely, and sometimes I feel his energy here around me. It's kinder than I would have guessed, and gentle, tender. Also a little sad."

"The music," Beverly said.

"I think so." Katie smiled. "It stirs the air. Also seems to calm things, sometimes. I never know for sure. After the previous visitor left, I thought it would be really good to play something."

The man in red.

It felt like time for us to make our way to the upper floor. But there was one more thing I wanted to ask.

"Do you spend much time out on the land?"

"Like Eustacia Vye roaming Egdon Heath, you mean?" She chuckled, and shook her head. "You know, the whole thing was turned into a Christmas tree plantation a hundred years ago. Afforestation, that's what it was called. Conifers as far as you could see." I hadn't known about this, as Katie could tell from my face. "There's more. The military took over big chunks of the heath to use for firing ranges. One can't go near those areas. Then later, when the dual carriageway was being built, all the paths heading north from the heath were just chopped off right there at the edge where they met the new road."

"So the heath isn't really the heath anymore and you don't spend much time out on it."

"Exactly. But about twenty-five years ago, they started clearing some of the trees and rhododendron. Not too long ago they reintroduced heath-ponies to graze the scrub and keep it down. So it's better than it was. Should continue to recover, too. A few hundred years, maybe it'll be the way it was when Eustacia Vye lived here."

I thanked her and she told me to be careful on the steep staircase and uneven floors above.

"I didn't mean to be rude about your question," she said as we began to walk through Hardy's father's office beyond the living room. "I understand what you were asking. There is a mood to the heath some nights, for sure. It's still a restless, unsettled place for humans to be."

❦

The stairs led to the room where Hardy's sisters had lived. On the mantle over the fireplace I found a typed information sheet in a plastic sleeve, but there was little need to explain what we saw beyond the faux furnishings, framed embroidery, raggedy quilted blanket spread on the narrow bed, and thin rug at its edge. Though the cottage's spaces may have been considered ample by Victorian standards, life here was dense and privacy rare.

Being in this compressed room with its odd angles and bleak shadows made me aware of how wrong I was ever to think of our yurt as small. My writing space there had been quirkily shaped, and fitting square-edged desks and bookcases into a room with curved walls had been a challenge, but that room was as big as this, and this was sleeping and working and living and dreaming space for two: Mary, Hardy's affectionate, close companion throughout childhood, his confidante—only a year and a half younger—and Katharine, born when Hardy was sixteen. Neither ever married, living here or nearby for most of their long years.

Beverly lingered in the sisters' room, but I was glad to leave it and head for the central bedroom where Hardy had been born 172 years and 2 days ago. Except I turned the wrong way and walked nearly to the staircase before realizing what I'd done. I turned back and entered the parents' bedroom. In many ways, this was the spot I'd come to Dorset to find, Hardy's headwaters, little suspecting that by the time I got here Hardy would have already touched and spoken to me.

This was the room, that was the bed (well, maybe not *the* bed), that was the chestnut wood floor where he'd been thrown aside as dead and then saved by Lizzie Downing in the morning light streaming through that window. I felt a surge of emotion—sympathy, gratitude, relief— and reflexively blurted out the words "Kine Ahoara," an old Yiddish magical phrase meant to ward off the evil eye and protect a child or loved one. A blessing steeped in fear of the worst.

It surprised me. It surprised Thomas Hardy too, because I felt him lurch from the corner of the room and heard him gasp.

If he'd said "Something I missed" again, I think I would have guessed that the whole thing—the Dorchester episode, the sound of movement through Thorncombe Woods' underbrush, and now this— had been a gag, somebody's idea of a prank to play on the old guy from the States with his pretty wife. After all, at breakfast that morning back in Lulworth, I detected an ironic glance pass between the two young couples sitting at a nearby table. They'd overheard me babble about finally seeing Hardy's Wessex heartland, and suffered through my reading of excerpts to Beverly as she ate her eggs. Maybe they'd had enough of all the besotted literary tourists, or didn't like something I'd said about Hardy's use of rustic folk in *The Woodlanders*, their dialect and superstitious ways, and hired an actor to taunt me.

But Hardy didn't speak. Once he found his balance, he scrutinized my face and I tried to hold his gaze, but this second close-up and intimate contact with Hardy was unsettling for me. It didn't feel like the Visitations I'd experienced when we lived in the yurt, with so much space around me. He was making yet another kind of contact, too, with his stare rather than his hand. It felt direct and purposeful, though I couldn't figure out what that purpose was. After a few seconds, he bowed his head as though approving my use of ancient spells, took a quick look around the room, and disappeared.

I remembered my father speaking Yiddish with his brothers and occasionally with my mother when there were discussions I wasn't supposed to understand. One of the few times I can remember him laughing was when he listened to Yiddish jokes on the car radio while driving to our Sunday morning breakfasts. He had to pull over because his eyes had filled with tears. Yiddish was the language of his humor and for expressing his warmest, deepest, and most private family feelings. For release. It was a language I only spoke a few words of. But I remembered how to use it for protecting someone close.

I thought I'd blurted out "Kine Ahoara" to somehow bless and protect the infant Hardy, or the phantom Hardy who was not at rest. But maybe I used the phrase, without being aware of it, to bless and protect myself as this journey of homage grew more focused and weird, became more of a search.

Guessing Hardy might have gone to his own bedroom, I followed. But it was empty except for the furnishings and bric-a-brac, and a breeze that stirred the curtains. I knew Hardy was no longer present. The view was west toward Black Down and the heath, and I sat on the window seat to see what he would have seen as he worked. I heard Beverly's footsteps in the hall. She stopped for a visit to the parents' room.

One of the most enduring images I have of Hardy—of the writer in his breakthrough years as a novelist—is the image of him observing, examining, watching. Mostly by himself, quiet, apart even in company, vigilant, noticing the world in its details. And this spot was where that habit had begun. I sat where he'd sat, and as I regarded what he'd grown up seeing, what he saw as he wrote his early books and found his way into the first great story, the tellingly titled *Far from the Madding Crowd*, I could see myself reflected in the windowpane. Graying hair and grizzled beard, a touch of wattle under the chin.

Yet at the same time there I was, age twenty-nine, driving from Springfield, Illinois, to Olympia, Washington, in my third cross-country relocation. It was July 1976, the country's bicentennial moment, town after town decked out in celebration just as England was now, in 2012, for the Queen's Jubilee. My daughter, nearing four years old, slept beside me on the front seat, head nodding as though in full agreement with the logic of her dream. I loved those long drives through the heartland with Becka beside me on the straight wide road. The trips were like dreams themselves. We seemed to be going nowhere at seventy miles per hour and I thought it all would never end: the road, the day, my child beside me, that fathering time in my life. On the back seat as we headed to Olympia, strapped in like another member of the family, was a huge box so stuffed that it bulged into my line of sight. What it was stuffed with were file folders—one for every poem or story I'd written, every draft, every letter of correspondence, every scrap of research—along with all the books and all the contributor's copies of obscure literary journals I couldn't bear to trust our movers to keep safe. At the front of the box, in the fattest folder, was a copy of my college honors thesis, a work most distinguished by its determined effort to track Hardy's struggle, in his novels, to leave the rural past behind while not abandoning his roots. Also by the number of *of*s in its title: "To Christminster: A Study of the Development of the Novels of Thomas Hardy." There was only one other copy of the thesis, stored somewhere in the library at Franklin and Marshall College along with every other honors thesis written in the college's long history. I had no idea why I'd kept my copy for the last seven years, why I was hauling it along with all the other excess paper, or what I would ever use it for. I hadn't opened the thing since defending it at my oral exams.

In the next breath, almost two years had passed and I was packing again, moving back across country and back to Springfield, Illinois. This time, though, I was being ruthless. The house we were moving into was seventy-five years old, and space for file storage and writing paraphernalia would be limited. It was time to jettison, to weed out. In the window of Thomas Hardy's bedroom, backgrounded by Egdon

Heath, I clearly saw myself in 1978, lifting the folder labeled HARDY THESIS, flipping the pages without really seeing them, and dumping it in a dark-green plastic trash bag along with so many other folders I would wish desperately to have back for the subsequent thirty-five years.

Then Beverly was there behind me. "Where have you been?" she whispered, letting me know she was present before running her hand gently against my neck and letting it rest on my shoulder. I told her about seeing Hardy again, and the journeys I'd just recalled. We stood together in Hardy's bedroom for a few minutes. I thought I heard Katie greet new visitors below, light laughter, a cough.

"I should read a Hardy novel," Beverly said as she looked around. "One he wrote here. One we haven't seen a movie of."

"There was a copy of *A Pair of Blue Eyes* for sale on the table downstairs. He wrote that after meeting Emma, while he was waiting to marry her."

"Is it dark?"

"Well, everybody rejects everybody else and the heroine flies in the end. I mean *dies* in the end." I glanced up and noticed the smoke alarm on the bare ceiling, directly above Hardy's bed. "But it has its lighter moments too."

We held hands as we walked to the hall's south end, where Hardy's grandmother had lived. I tried to imagine them all clomping around in this narrow corridor, parents shouting below, a storm of human need and urgency matched by winds howling off the heath. Something like that. The feeling here isn't cozy, I thought. Isn't easy. It's intimate but without intimacy. Stringent. And the quiet feels temporary. I know some of this is because family life is no longer lived here, because it's more of a museum than a home anymore. A display of life, not life itself, a stage set for a canceled play. And it's of a different time, a largely lost way of existence. But what I felt came from deeper than all that, from a spirit or its absence that remained in the air.

Back downstairs, Katie was busy with an elderly couple and a bored adolescent who must have been their grandson. We squeezed by them for a quick look at the kitchen and larder, then returned to the front door. I mouthed the word *Thanks*, and Katie waved in response. Outside, a pair of volunteers worked in the garden. A few weeks from now, the place would be gaudy with color.

Instead of going through Thorncombe Woods again, Beverly and I walked to our car on the narrow lane Hardy knew as Cherry Alley. He also knew it as Veterans' Valley after all the retired military people who'd lived in cottages lining the way. But the buildings and most of the trees were gone, the old well that served the lane was covered over in ivy, and the look was now of a prosperous country development with farm buildings and newish homes. I turned around for a final glimpse of Hardy's cottage. The hedge around it and the elevation of our position made it so all I could see was the very top of the central chimney and smoke being absorbed into the hazy air.

5

I noticed the wall decor as soon as we stepped into the tea room. There were framed book jackets from a dozen foreign-language editions of *Tess of the D'Urbervilles*, a map of Hardy's fictional Wessex region with Tess's wanderings highlighted in thick black lines, pencil sketches of Stonehenge and of Hardy at fifty composing the novel, and stills from at least five film versions. The shop was named Tea Is for Tess, so I'd expected some kitschy references to the character—Tess teapots or tea towels or T-shirts, maybe a few generic paintings of Tess-related landscapes—but this was a joyous and specific riot of appreciation. I peered at a bookshelf near the front door, stacked two-deep with battered old hardback copies of the novel. Another shelf held a scale model, knit from local yarns, of the Pure Drop Inn where readers first meet the character of Tess Durbeyfield in Hardy's pages.

The proprietor watched my reactions and chuckled as she walked over. She stood with us and gazed around as we did. I said a solid American "Wow."

"That group of glossies by the long table there come from the 1979 film." She pointed and flicked her finger each time she said a name: "Nastassja Kinski. Peter Firth. Ahh, he was a good-looking one. Next to him, John Collin. Leigh Lawson. Caught the nasty side of Alec d'Urberville, all right. One on the end is Roman Polanski."

She directed our attention to the back corner of the room. "That bunch by the loo are from the London Weekend Television version. Nineteen ninety-eight. Three-hour program it was, and brilliant. Not sure if you got it over in the States. Oliver Milburn, bit of a heartthrob, he played Angel Clare. Was actually a Dorset man. Played it just right, sensitive and selfish both. You see him in everything now. *Wuthering Heights. Coronation Street.* Almost forty—how time passes."

She shook her head and lifted a hand to her mouth as though trying to stanch the flow of words. Then she picked up menus, led us to a small table by the side window, and began straightening out place settings. When she was done, and saw that we were still standing to peruse the photos, she slapped her hands together in quick applause.

"This wall are all from the BBC-TV miniseries. Hard to believe it was four years ago already. There you have Gemma Arterton, Tess. Eddie Redmayne was Angel Clare. What a cutie. Hans Matheson was your Alec. See that May Day Parade scene in the middle? Woman in the green dress standing on Dancing Ledge with the sea frothing behind her? That would be me."

"You?" Beverly leaned closer to the photo, studied it, looked back. "Yes, it sure is."

"That was one very long day. I loved every minute of it. Didn't feel like an Extra at all, never bored, never tired. Dream come true."

"But you must have been very cold."

She shrugged. "Didn't feel it at all." She pulled back Beverly's chair and said, "By the way, I'm Sharon. My niece Chloe will serve you. But do call me if you need anything."

"Before you go," Beverly said, "can you tell us which dishes are gluten-free?"

We'd planned for this lunch six months ago. Actually, Beverly had done most of the planning—otherwise we risked ending up in Dorset Vermont or Dorset Minnesota, having gotten there by way of Acapulco and Tallahassee—and as she researched and arranged our itinerary, the central problem for each day was where to eat safely.

Exposure to gluten wouldn't kill her, but it would trigger a series of inflammatory reactions in her gut and throughout her musculoskeletal system that would virtually immobilize her. We'd seen the results: four years ago, she'd been a certified master gardener who'd had to give up gardening because it hurt too much to stand and bend and lift, been a painter of landscapes who'd had to give up painting because she couldn't work at her easel anymore. When her physical therapist suggested she try eliminating gluten from her diet, she felt better so quickly that we committed ourselves to it and never wavered.

I gave up gluten, too. I knew, as a New Yorker who craved sesame bagels and Hawaiian pizzas and thick crusty heroes, that it might be difficult, but I wanted to act out of solidarity with Beverly. Eating gluten-free was something I could join and support her in, as she had joined and supported me in my life with brain damage, marrying me, loving me, sharing her deeply private home world with me. Besides, as the family's cook I knew there was a risk, if I didn't give it up, of contaminating her food with gluten from my own.

Her pain resolved, she got stronger, fitter. It was a joy to see her move like Beverly again. And I lost eighteen pounds and my cholesterol dropped 25 percent. How fitting that a small sacrifice done out of love— a kind of speaking my heart—should end up directly benefiting my heart. We seldom ate in restaurants anymore because there were so few we could trust to be rigorous enough about gluten. Which made travel risky, and explains why Beverly spent hour after hour studying British restaurants, inns, B&Bs, grocery stores. And why she was elated to find Tea Is for Tess.

It was located in the historic market town of Wareham, near Poole Harbor and the coast, in the heart of what Hardy called South Wessex. When Beverly found it on the Internet, located it on Google Maps, and zoomed in for a satellite view, she called me over to her computer. The words "Enjoy our gluten-free menu" were clearly visible on a sign beside the door. The menu was even available online. We'd been looking forward to it as a great treat. Worry-free food! That's a big deal in the life of people on restricted diets.

In his work, Hardy had transformed Wareham into Anglebury and sent Thomasin Yeobright to Anglebury in her failed attempt to marry Damon Wildeve at the start of *The Return of the Native*. If Thomasin could get there easily enough by foot and wagon from her home at Blooms-End—the cottage at Higher Bockhampton—then Beverly and I in our zippy rental car could detour ten minutes out of our way to eat at Tea Is for Tess. Gluten-free and Hardy-obsessed. I don't know how it gets much better than that.

Distracted, pouting, Chloe brought us two new menus and removed the ones Sharon had given us. "Everything on this one's okay," she said. Then she stood there, waiting to take our order, drumming her pencil tip against the pad in her left hand. She seemed harried even though there was only one other occupied table. She looked around, looked up and down, anywhere but at us as she bobbed her head and moved her lips to some inner song. I thought she resembled a young Kate Winslet from the movie version of *Jude the Obscure*, then realized I needed to stop imagining everyone I encountered as characters in Hardy movies.

I ordered prawn salad with the British incarnation of Thousand Island dressing, Marie Rose sauce. Though I was hungry, I needed a light entrée because what I'd been longing for, from the moment I'd seen the online menu, was the first gluten-free cream tea I'd ever had. Scones, for God's sake. Apple Crumble and Treacle Sponge Pudding. Wanted to leave plenty of room for that. Beverly, thinking the same way, ordered a cheese and leek quiche, which was prepared with an almond flour crust.

"Cream tea," she said. "I've been dreaming about this."

"Did I ever tell you about the time my mother took me to the Russian Tea Room in New York?"

"Yes, you have. Many times. But tell me again."

"I must have been seven or eight because we still lived in Brooklyn and took the subway. It was up on Fifty-Seventh Street and the inside was enormous. Huge chandelier, paintings everywhere, samovars on tables, people in furs, tailored suits. Snooty waiters."

"I bet she asked to change tables, right? Too much breeze, too much light? Show those big shots who they were dealing with."

"Of course. Changed tables twice. By the time we were served I was so afraid of spilling something and getting whacked that I could hardly eat, which pissed her off even more than if I'd spilled. She'd ordered some pastries with cream and confectioner's sugar. No way to eat it without making a mess. She just sat there seething."

"So you were trapped. In trouble if you eat, in trouble if you don't."

"Right. Plus the waiter didn't bring the food fast enough and the busboy tried to clear the table too soon. She was exactly where she most wanted to be and responded by being more and more furious. But God, I loved that tea for some reason. I must've had three cups. Tea in a restaurant! I took it upon myself to compliment the waiter. When he left the table my mother grabbed my hand and squeezed. 'Shut up, you *pisher*. You have nothing to say. Never did and never will.'"

"No matter how many times I hear that story, it shocks me."

"I don't think I ordered tea in a restaurant from 1955 until we got to England two weeks ago. I can't believe how good it feels to do that."

"And now you've not only ordered tea, you've ordered gluten-free cream tea. In England, home of the poshest of accents. Your mother would . . . what's that word?"

"Plotz."

Sharon came back to our table. I thought—dreaded—that she was going to say the cream tea wasn't available. But, and I can still feel how relieved it made me, she'd come back to tell Beverly it would take a few minutes for the quiche to be ready. And to talk some more about Hardy.

"You're into Hardy, aren't you?" she said. "Can tell right off when real fans come in."

"My husband is," Beverly said. "The plots are too grim for me."

Sharon accepted that with a quick dip of her head. "Particularly Tess, I'd imagine," she said, leaning back to laugh, "and Jude, too. Grim is the right word. No wonder he stopped writing novels after that one. I mean, how much further into the dark could he go?" Then she reached over to touch my arm and said, "Here's the question I like to ask, if you don't mind. The answer tells me a lot about someone. What's your favorite thing that Hardy wrote?"

"Whoa. That's a hard one." I'd read *The Mayor of Casterbridge* at several points in my life, but it wasn't my favorite. Too much coincidence and contrivance, and the suicidal conclusion. And *Jude the Obscure*, which ironically had brought me so much hope, was too hyperdark and fatalistic to be a favorite book. "I can usually respond to almost any of his stuff. But I do draw the line at *The Dynasts*," I said.

"Well, that tells me what's your least favorite, and welcome to the club. I've met only a handful of people who've even managed to finish *The Dynasts*. But what about the one you love?"

"Well, take away the heavy-handed ending and all the moralizing, I think *Two on a Tower* is the one that flat-out moves me the most."

"I see." Sharon nodded. "So you like a real love story."

"I've been thinking about that a lot since we got to Dorset."

"Love stories?"

"Hardy and love, yes." I took a sip of water. "What he got, what he missed."

Sharon looked around the shop, lowering her voice. "Love wasn't easy for him, was it? In his books or in his life." She was silent for a moment, thinking about what she wanted to say next. "How much do you know about his life?"

"Just what's in the biographies, and the Life he ghostwrote. Plus the poetry and fiction, of course."

"Then you know about Tryphena?"

"His Sparks cousin?"

She waited to see if I would say anything more. The other couple in the shop got up to leave, thanking Sharon on their way out. Because of how quickly and steadily she'd been speaking, Sharon's silence seemed ominous, like sudden cacophony on a film score.

"Perhaps," she said.

"Perhaps his cousin?"

"There are those who say she was something more."

"You mean his lover?"

"That, too. But some say she was also closer than a cousin. That she was the illegitimate daughter of his mother's illegitimate daughter, actually."

"So, his niece," Beverly said. "And his lover."

"He probably didn't know they were more than cousins till later," Sharon said, "when he gave her a ring and the family went mad."

Beverly looked at me. I knew what she was thinking: another recipient of the ring.

"And then he broke the relationship off?" I asked. I hadn't remembered any of this from the biographies. Hardy's stern mother had an illegitimate daughter? Who in turn had one of her own, who grew up to be Hardy's lover? That came dangerously close to soap-opera territory. Or the plot of a potential Thomas Hardy novel.

Perhaps this incestuous connection was what he'd missed—the fact that the woman he loved was so closely related. "Or did Tryphena break it off? Or was there something like a family conclave?"

Sharon didn't answer. Instead, she left the table and disappeared into the kitchen, returning with our salad and quiche on a tray alongside a copy of Hardy's *Complete Poems*. She served our meal, told us to enjoy it, and left the book for us to peruse. "Page 62," she said. "Thoughts of Phena, At News of Her Death."

Instead of reaching for the fork, I took my pen from my pocket and stopped myself just before sticking it into the salad. As we ate, I kept rereading the poem until certain phrases began to grab hold. Hearing of Tryphena's death, thinking about how long they'd been out of touch and how little he'd known of her life after they parted, her marriage and children, her years in Devon, Hardy called her his "lost prize" and recognized that he retained only "the phantom of the maiden of yore." She haunted him, but only in the form of her early years, the years when they'd been close. Sure, it could mean that this phantom, this lost prize, was more to him than simply a cousin. Those are intense ways to recall her. But it didn't prove anything, on its own.

Sharon returned to clear away our plates and make certain we still wanted our cream teas. When we said we did, she nodded to Chloe, who went into the kitchen. "I'll just say one more thing, since you did mention your interest in Hardy and love. There are those say he based all his great heroines on Tryphena. The whole tragic lot of them, lost to love. Never did stop writing about her in his novels."

She left us again, and we reached across the table to hold hands. Beverly said, "That can't be the thing that haunts him still—being unaware they were uncle and niece—it has to be even deeper than that."

Chloe brought out a pot of tea and a plate of scones with jams and clotted cream. The scones looked so fluffy I had to smile. At last, someone's figured out how to bake a gluten-free scone that rises. It was at least four inches thick.

Beverly examined hers and said, "Oh no!"

"What's wrong?"

"Stretch marks." She pointed to the scone I'd picked up and torn open. "Look at it. Have you ever seen a gluten-free dough that rose like this?"

"Maybe Sharon has a secret about that, too?" But I knew Beverly was right. And I knew her radar was infallible when it came to this stuff.

"No way it's gluten-free," she said.

We called Chloe back. "Yeah," she said, "it's okay to eat."

Beverly picked up our plates and walked past Chloe to the kitchen area. When she returned, empty-handed, she said, "Sharon almost passed out when I showed her the scones. Chloe, apparently, is having an off day. Snatched the wrong ones to serve us."

When Sharon brought the gluten-free scones, they were only a little less flat than matzoh. We had no doubt about them being gluten-free. She was mortified, and told us there would be no charge for the cream tea. The mistake was, she said, quoting *Tess of the D'Urbervilles*, the ill-judged execution of the well-judged plan of things.

As though in compensation, she stood by the table and said, "Since we were talking about Hardy's lost love, did you know there are people who believe Tryphena bore Hardy a child?"

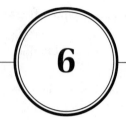

6

We got into the car and sat there staring through the windshield at the exterior of Tea Is for Tess. Its skin was a little chapped from the wind, but otherwise the building looked solid and sound. It was real. Breeze ruffled bunting strung for the Jubilee celebration. A sturdy gray Vauxhall turned in from the street and parked by the "Enjoy our gluten-free menu" sign. The driver was neither dressed in Victorian garb nor resembled Thomas Hardy. I was feeling the need to verify such things.

I hadn't had the presence of mind to question Sharon about what she'd said. Just started spreading jam on my disk of fluffless scone and nodded as though it made perfect sense to me that Tryphena Sparks had given birth to Hardy's child. Perfect sense that she was eleven years younger than her baby's father, who was at best her cousin, at worst her uncle. Tidy Thomas Hardy with a secret life almost as messy as Lord Bryon's.

When we paid our bill, Sharon thanked us, told us the weather promised to be fine, and wished us well. It was almost as though she understood I'd need time to process what she'd given us.

I put the key in the ignition, but still didn't start the car. "Hardy and Tryphena had a child," I said. "What's next, we find out he had a secret twin named Tim?"

"Is this the first you've heard of a child?"

"I'm not sure. After Sharon said that, I vaguely remembered a child coming up in the biographies but being dismissed as bogus. I think there was something about a gay relationship too, with a friend who later killed himself. All unsubstantiated gossip. I guess I didn't pay much attention to any of it, and it didn't stick."

"We've already heard the one about Tryphena being the love child of his mother's love child. If what Sharon said is true, we've got a third generation of love children."

"Plus all those other flirtations, like with Cassie Pole. I don't know, it fits and it doesn't. He comes across as this detached fuddy-duddy who spent a lot of time in his room writing. Staid, old hands-off Hardy. But then there's all the love-related torment in his work. His totally overt furtive maneuvers. His own record of all the women across the years who obsessed him."

"And this family tradition of love children we keep hearing about."

"Which would explain that zeal for secretiveness. This is the guy who burned all his papers and self-ghostwrote a biography in which a lot of key years and key people were left out. Maybe those were the years of the child in his life. Or maybe being with his child is what he missed, for some reason. If there was a child, did it survive? Was Hardy in its life? I keep thinking about the tragic child in *Jude the Obscure* who kills his half siblings and then hangs himself. I need to do some serious reading when we get home."

"I'm beginning to understand why Hardy's spirit might not be at rest." Beverly leaned her head back against the seat and took a deep breath. "I'm tired. Let's go back to the room and take a nap before we do the coast walk."

We drove toward the B&B in West Lulworth. The tight rural road we were on, B3070, twisted across the River Frome and West Holme Heath, and took us near an army firing range where signs warned of "Sudden Gunfire" and "Tanks Crossing." Soon it narrowed further and entered a tight dark zigzag of overhanging trees. I slowed and kept to the center of the road, knowing Beverly was thinking the same thing I was: Remember Penzance.

On our way from Crantock to Land's End last week, we'd been on a road just like this when a gleaming black Land Rover suddenly filled the road ahead, coming right at us. I veered left and hadn't been able to see a mound of dirt at the blind edge. I drove over it fast enough and the mound was substantial enough that we both thought the car was going to flip. Which was only a warm-up for the return trip through Penzance, when another burly vehicle—a van, this time—burst into another long narrow tunnel between high hedgerows. This time a hidden jutting rock jolted and slashed our front left tire. The jarring was so thorough, the sound so loud, we were sure the car's chassis had been mangled and the wheel destroyed. Beverly screamed, then laughed with relief at finding us still alive. I pulled over and we assessed the damage. The impact had been confined to the tire and wheel. The rubber was profoundly gouged in two places, with flaps like torn skin revealing the inner tire wall, but it wasn't flat. Wasn't even leaking air. Beverly nudged the flaps back into place but we knew they weren't likely to stay.

Before we'd arrived in England, I imagined the great challenge would be driving on the wrong side of the road with the steering wheel on the wrong side of the car and the gear shift on the wrong side of the steering wheel. But that turned out to be manageable, if never quite natural. The great challenge was the absurdly narrow roads edged by concealed brick walls and sharp protruding rock, gouged with potholes, lacking lane markings, distorted by shadows out of which speeding vehicles bolted and gave no ground, festooned with roundabouts, and lined with confusing and contradictory road signs. I'd read in the *Daily Mail* that at one junction near Oldham, motorists are told not to turn left, not to turn right, to give way, and to keep to the 40 mph speed limit—all at the same time. It all made "Sudden Gunfire" and "Tanks Crossing" seem like benign notices. To drive British roads was to enter an arena of pandemonium where cutting-edge automobile technology met medieval road designs and neolithic human combat impulses. I needed to nap any day I did a lot of driving.

By the time we reached the B&B, I had to gather myself before entering the property. The building was stone and built in 1871, before anyone was planning to accommodate cars. Pulling into its small parking lot required you to swing out into the oncoming lane of rushing traffic, make a sharp turn off the road, squeeze through an opening barely wide enough for a horse-drawn cabriolet, and veer up a steep slope without damaging the bottom of the car. Exiting backwards—the only way out—was even trickier. I didn't want to think about doing that again.

⇌

When we entered the B&B, the owners were sitting in their dining room having tea. Anthony Swain stood and waved us over. Lean and fit in his late fifties, with crisply parted gray hair and a careful balance of reserve and bonhomie, he was retired from the military and still charmed by the novelty of running a B&B. And when he needed a break, he'd told us that morning, he went to look at the sea. "Go every day," he said. "You never lose that after so many years as a navy man."

Nan, with a voice like Julia Childs and a smile like Julia Roberts, had confessed right away that having her Anthony home all the time was a blessing, except when it wasn't, and they'd both laughed at that. "Not much for the hoover or the omelet pan, our Anthony, but ask him about Dorset history or literature or the best places to walk, and he'll go on forever."

It had been Anthony who'd told us that we mustn't miss the coast walk to Durdle Door. "Just down the road a bit, then walk across the field along Hambury Tout, and when you run out of land you'll catch sight of the thing down below." He'd said it was a limestone arch left when the sea drilled through the softer rock—"That's how it got its name, *Durdle* being the Old English word for drill"—and the footpath between Lulworth Cove and Durdle Door was far and away the busiest in all southwest England because people flocked to see that thing. "Jurassic Coast. Unspoiled. Except where it's spoiled."

When I'd said I knew Thomas Hardy had included a key scene at Lulworth Cove in *Far from the Madding Crowd*, and I wanted to see the spot, Anthony had actually applauded. "A Hardy man! I knew it. They shot scenes right out there when they made the film. Julie Christie stayed here, you know. Before we owned it. At least that's what they told us."

"So," Anthony said now, when we joined them in the dining room, "any Hardy sightings?"

Beverly and I looked at each other. Holy cow! No way I was going to tell him about what had happened in Dorchester's South Street and the Hardy cottage. I wondered if Anthony's phrasing was just a local expression for Hardy sites, and not literally about sighting Hardy. Or who knows, maybe I wasn't the only one who saw him. Maybe there was a Zombie Hardy at large.

"After Dorchester and Higher Bockhampton," I said, "we went over to Wareham for lunch and cream tea at a shop where they serve gluten-free."

As Beverly and I had just done, Anthony and Nan looked at each as though saying Holy cow! Then Anthony sat back down and said, "So you've met our Sharon Taylor, then?"

"She was very gracious."

"And told you all about appearing in the Tess film," Nan said, and chuckled.

I nodded. "We loved seeing all the memorabilia."

"And then she somehow got around to Mr. Hardy and his cousin Tryphena, am I right?" Anthony said.

"And baby Randall," Nan added. "Let's not forget Randy."

"Named perhaps for his alleged father's alleged lustfulness, eh?"

"So you don't buy it?" Beverly asked.

"No one's ever found a shred of evidence. Just gossip and 'proof' drawn out of various bits in the poems and such. Rubbish, that's what it is. Do you know where the rumor comes from?"

"I just know the biographies I've read thought it was spurious."

Anthony nodded. "Spurious indeed. The 'source' is Tryphena's demented daughter Nellie when the poor thing was almost ninety and being led on to say all sorts of silliness by some Hardy crackpot."

"Tryphena had a daughter?"

"She did. And three sons. Married a pub owner from Devon named Bromell. Died at thirty-nine, poor girl."

"But not a child with Hardy?"

"As I said, no evidence whatsoever. No records, documents, family lore. And people in the villages were chatty, all right, knew everyone's story and told it widely. Just like today. Couldn't hush a thing like that up."

"We feel it's our duty," Nan said, "to protect Mr. Hardy's reputation from people like that. If you go back to her shop, I guarantee Sharon will offer another tidbit. Hardy abandoned Randy, or if she's feeling especially feisty, Hardy murdered his child."

"And then show you a poem that proves it."

"Or a passage in the Tess novel," Nan said. She reached for her husband's drained teacup and placed it beside her own, ready to get back to work but not ready to leave the conversation. "Anthony's done a lot of research on Mr. Hardy since guests are always asking after him."

Anthony shook his head. "There are a lot of Hardy cranks out there."

"Daft. We want to be sure you know what's true."

"I appreciate that." Beverly and I stood up to leave. But there was something I needed to get clear. "Anthony, a little while ago you asked if we'd had any Hardy sightings. What did you mean by 'sightings'?"

He blinked, exchanged a quick glance with Nan, smiled, and said, "Why, what did you think I meant? A ghost?"

"I was struck by the word."

"Only a figure of speech, I assure you. But it is true that we've had more than one guest who claimed they saw an apparition of Thomas Hardy during their time in Dorset."

"Especially around Max Gate," Nan said. "In the grove of trees Mr. Hardy planted—the Nut Walk—or over by the little cemetery where he and Mrs. Hardy buried their dear pets. How Mr. Hardy loved that dreary place!"

"On the heath, too, don't forget," Anthony said. "People see Hardy there as well. And Stinsford Churchyard. Really, where hasn't the phantom of Thomas Hardy been sighted?"

"Thing is, people want to see him so badly they somehow manage to succeed. And we've just gotten used to opening the way for them to talk about it if we know they're into Mr. Hardy."

"Hospitality," Anthony said. "We want our guests to be comfortable."

"And properly informed."

"Yes, properly informed." Now Anthony stood and picked up the teapot along with the cups Nan had gathered. "So what about it, then? Any Hardy sightings?"

Were Anthony and Nan right, was that what I'd done? Conjured up Hardy because I needed to see him after all the years of reading and having a feeling for his work, of imagining and in some respects of loving him? I hadn't thought so, given my long history with Visitations, including Visits from people for whom I felt no love (Rasputin, or Tsar Nicholas II of Russia) or whose work I admired but didn't keep returning to as I did to Hardy's (Ezra Pound, Paul Gauguin, the Irish poet Patrick Kavanagh). I seldom thought about the Visitors before they arrived, was always taken by surprise. What the hell was the Tsar doing at the edge of our garden picking mushrooms! This was the guy who drove my grandparents out of their homes. Why did I need Robert Frost to tell me to chop more pine for the woodpile? Today's Visitation from Hardy felt like those in the way it seemed to come from outside myself, not from me. If that wasn't true, then it came from a place in me that I wasn't in touch with.

But maybe that was changing now. As Beverly had suggested, maybe something in me was prompting Hardy's Visitations. Was there, in fact, something I missed that only he could lead me to? Well, to discover that, I knew I still had to find out what Hardy missed.

Anthony had been honest, so I said, "Yes, a Hardy sighting. Two sightings, actually. And a tap on my shoulder. And he spoke to me."

"Spoke to you?" Anthony glanced at Nan and raised his eyebrows.

"What I think he said was 'Something I missed.'"

"Well, what do you make of that!"

"I'm asking myself the same thing."

7

We closed the curtains, but despite the softened light and my exhaustion I couldn't fall asleep. Might have been because of all the PG Tips I'd drunk at lunch, or the conversation we'd just had with our hosts. Might have been because I kept seeing Hardy's image on various signs along the road, and fingerposts pointing to Thomas Hardy's cottage or Thomas Hardy's Max Gate or a footpath called the Hardy Way, and was waiting for the man himself to make another Visitation. Or because of all the information about him I was trying to absorb, coming at me from so many angles.

Beverly, usually more sensitive to caffeine than I am, slept beside me, lips slightly parted, eyes slightly open, and I tried to imagine her dreaming of the gardens we'd been to in England. I thought of walking with her through the Botanical Gardens in Oxford and in Wales, Hidcote in the Cotswolds, Lanhydrock in Cornwall. We couldn't get to every garden she'd hoped to visit, but what we saw was nourishing to her spirit. The gardens made her happy the way bird-watching did, and I could see—actually see—the outpouring of love in her eyes. I know: first he sees Visitors, now he claims to see love flow. When imagining Beverly's dreams and her joy didn't get me to sleep, and neither did memories of soaking together in our wood-burning hot tub in the years before the well went dry, I tried to match her steady breathing. But I still couldn't relax, couldn't stop my racing thoughts.

It was poignant, but also gloomy and predictable—Hardyesque—to see how his desperate secretiveness merely kindled gossip and rumors like those about his lovers, his sexuality, his fathering of a child. He would have been, and perhaps still was, horrified at the intrusion into his privacy, the provocative, scandalous insinuations. Particularly if they were true and he hadn't succeeded in containing their spread. Maybe that's what he missed: how to remain hidden. But surely Hardy had known, in that cunning mind of his, that what he'd hoped to conceal would eventually be revealed. Or that even worse matters would be fabricated. Because central to his beliefs was the idea that man's deepest desires were fated to be thwarted. And secrets revealed. "All her shining keys will be took from her," he'd written about a woman who had just died, "and her cupboards opened; and little things 'a didn't wish seen, anybody will see; and her wishes and ways will all be as nothing!"

A poem of Hardy's was on my mind, the early, gnarled sonnet about love with the bitter title "Revulsion." This was the poem, written in his midtwenties, where he said it would be better not to love, better "to fail obtaining love," because love was certain to fail. By winning love we win the risk of losing it. And, in Hardy's view, losing love hurts more than he can bear, hurts like a violent gash, like being torn apart, its pain worse than whatever pleasure might come from loving.

What makes a man, even a young man posing as world-weary or love-savvy, think this way? I'd recently read a commencement address given at Kenyon College by the novelist Jonathan Franzen in which he said, "The prospect of pain generally, the pain of loss, of breakup, of death, is what makes it so tempting to avoid love." But while Franzen knows love is worth the risk, he also understands what that risk truly is: "To love a specific person, and to identify with their struggles and joys as if they were your own, you have to surrender some of your self." This—surrendering himself—may be precisely the thing Thomas Hardy couldn't bring himself to do. The thing he feared to chance.

What I was learning about Hardy was whirling around itself and tangling with what I'd already known, with my memories of his work, my feeling of his imminence. Since there were so many gaps in the record, sorting rumor and fact wasn't going to be enough, even if it were possible, even if my cognitive powers were up to the task. The Truth about Hardy and what he may have missed, such as it was, might yet be Hardy's to reveal.

I began to think about the most clear-headed, rigorous, demanding investigator I knew, and how she might approach untangling these elements to see how Hardy's story fit together. I'm certainly no reporter or literary journalist, but my daughter is. Rebecca is forty, and after the publication of her book *The Immortal Life of Henrietta Lacks*, a best seller for three years now, she seemed like an overnight success. But my God, how long and hard she'd worked. She'd thought about the story of Henrietta Lacks and the Lacks family since she was a teenager, studied biological science in college, and devoted ten years to researching and writing the book, overcoming the resistance and misdirection of her subjects, always going deeper, following leads, interviewing, checking and rechecking facts. There were times when she didn't let me know where the story led her, the backroads in the South, wrecked slave shacks, snake- and tick-infested graveyards and tobacco fields, or alone at night on the streets of inner-city Baltimore. She knew I'd be wild with worry over the risks she took, the pain she absorbed, the angry and sometimes dangerous people she met with, eventually calming and winning them over. To find the truth about an unknown black tobacco farmer, whose cancerous cells—taken without her knowledge—became one of medicine's most essential and lucrative tools even though her family remained unable to afford health care, Rebecca had to earn the trust of the family as well as the scientists involved. It was grueling, sometimes disheartening work, but she understood its value and power, and never wavered, never rushed. It was an inspiring model for solving the kind of jumbled mystery of *what happened* . . . She had been chasing phantoms . . . Everywhere and nowhere . . . We were colleagues, we were friends, I was extraordinarily lucky . . . When she was a toddler I remember Becka pursuing a squirrel in the backyard, falling and getting back up, not crying, not stopping, chasing falling getting up . . .

⟱

Thomas Hardy was pedaling a bicycle on the narrow road ahead as we drove around a curve. I recognized his costly Rover Cobb bike from photos taken of Hardy in his sixties. He wore a wide straw hat, knee-length cycling pants from which long black socks descended into thick black shoes, and a jacket that flapped in the wind. Though I could only see him from behind, I knew he had on a vest and tie. The bike was red and so was our car, vivid as cardinals in the landscape.

A woman was riding beside him at the margin of the road. As Hardy gestured to her, his balance wavered but held. I couldn't distinguish the woman's features, but she was tall and thin and from the way she moved, the way she sat, seemed youthful. High-spirited. She looked straight ahead, focused, poised. Her passage scattered thrushes from the bordering trees.

Soon the road shrank, hedges looming, expanding as though breathing. Everything darkened, and the riders entered another curve. I slowed. We passed a sign pointing in all four directions and saying "Stinsford Churchyard, Thomas Hardy's Grave." The road was now a rutted clay lane at dusk, like an ancient pathway for horse-drawn carts. Hardy turned his face to the right, looking directly at his companion, and I could see the swoop of his waxed mustache tip, a flash of white material above his jacket collar.

Then I heard a roar like an approaching tornado. It was a sound I knew well from the thirteen years I'd lived in Illinois. The pea-soup sky, the electric odor, and heavy gasping air. Still the cyclists continued, oblivious, and now there was a small child riding behind Hardy. In a flash the three of them began to spiral and swirl, caught up in the storm. But the storm wasn't a storm at all, it had transformed into an onrushing vehicle the size and shape of a giant Humvee, black, so wide it overlapped both edges of the lane. Beverly was pulling on my arm, pulling me from the car, pulling me from the dream.

I lay there panting, unwilling to move my eyes from hers till I was sure where the dream ended and reality began. I got up and wrote in my notebook for a few minutes. It wasn't just that the dream was so vivid, or that it reflected how fully Hardy had entered my immediate experience within the space of the few hours since he'd touched my shoulder in Dorchester. It was the sense that I felt responsible now, in ways I didn't yet understand, for whatever had been entrusted to me by his Visitation. I felt the stakes escalating, at least for me, and maybe in some way for Hardy too, for his spirit at large in the world.

When I finished writing about the dream, I remembered what had crossed my mind just before falling asleep. Thoughts of Becka as a child had been flooding back lately, as I neared my sixty-fifth birthday and as she moved ever more fully into the world. Most of those thoughts had to do with simple, everyday life, often food-related—nothing about the moments to suggest they would remain embedded in memory, would survive the damage to areas of my brain that control memory. But they were there, etched into the core of my self, the essence of my being, the heart of my story. My daughter standing on a stool beside me at the stove, a spatula in her hand, in charge of cooking chicken Marsala, gently testing the meat for doneness. Kneading oat bread at the age of five, looking at her gooey hands and the splatters of dough on the window beside her and saying "everything's just fine." Experimenting with non-traditional coatings and shapes for the bagels she was making from scratch. Weekday mornings when she was in elementary school we'd go out for breakfast together before I dropped her off. I loved listening to her talk, how quick her mind was, how playful. Ordinary moments in the life of a father, though there wouldn't have been such moments in my father's life. Or in Thomas Hardy's life. Etched into the core of himself, the essence of his being, the heart of his story.

⇇

While I was writing those notes, Beverly opened the laptop and googled Tryphena Sparks and Randy. She read for a few minutes. "Come see this," she said.

My daughter's wasn't the only tenacious, clear-thinking, logical mind I relied on. Before Beverly was an artist or gardener or hospice social worker, she'd been a scientist—a geologist—and brought a scientist's trained approach to making sense of the evidence. I'd tried—even before brain damage altered my cognitive powers—to do the same, but I was no match for either Beverly or Becka when it came to focused complexity of thought, memory systems, logic, abstract reasoning.

There were about a dozen windows open on Beverly's laptop screen and she was shaking her head. "Anthony had it right," she said. "Looks like there's a book we'll have to find for you. *Providence and Mr. Hardy*, it's called. Written by Lois Deacon and Terry Coleman. Deacon seems to be the one who sat down a bunch of times with Tryphena's daughter Eleanor, or Nellie, in, let's see, in 1965." She switched windows and said, "Then there's a book on Hardy by a Robert Gittings that demolishes the whole Deacon argument about Tryphena and the existence of a secret child." She switched windows again. "Here's a picture of Tryphena. I really wanted to see what she looked like, didn't you?"

I did, though I hadn't thought of it till Beverly brought it up. She enlarged the image and we studied it. Tryphena was dressed in a ruffled white wedding gown, sitting with her right hand to her cheek, her calm face gazing directly at the camera, its expression savvy, almost wry, acknowledging but hardly overwhelmed by the gravity of the ritual and discipline of the ceremonial photograph. She looked willing to be there, but not particularly emotional about it. Like her heart and soul were elsewhere.

"Wow," I whispered. "It's like she's just waiting. Like she knows the ending and it's up to us to find our way there."

"If we're going to do that, it's time to ask what we really know at this point."

"I think there are three twined mysteries. My mistake so far has been trying to think about all of them at once. I have enough trouble just thinking about one thing at once." I started flipping through my notes. "First there's the old mystery of what really happened in Hardy's love life. Who did he love and when did he love her?" I thought of my dream, the woman I couldn't recognize riding beside Hardy, the sudden appearance of the child. "If the gist of the Hardy-Tryphena stories is right—kid or no kid—then it seems like he allowed himself when he was in his late twenties, early thirties, to lose the one woman he truly loved. Then right away he married Emma, a woman for whom he couldn't sustain love. When she died, he made a marriage of convenience with Florence, who was young enough to be his daughter."

"I found something he wrote in a letter about marrying Florence," Beverly said, looking back at her laptop. "Listen to this: 'Having known each other so many years, & having been long associated in literary doings, we thought this step would be prosy and formal to a degree.' Romantic, huh?"

"Prosy and formal. That's pretty cold."

"Did he give his heart to anyone, really? All the covering up, and the conflicting stories."

"So that's one mystery: What's real, what's false in Hardy's love life? And, you know, am I going to be the one who solves it all?" We looked at each other, and I knew the answer: Well, maybe I can offer a credible story about what Hardy meant by what he'd said to me. "Then there's the mystery of why the Visitation happened. Why he came to me, as you asked."

"And why now?"

"I've been thinking about both of those things. Maybe there is no reason why he came to me, or came to me now—maybe he's been going around saying 'Something I missed' to lots of people who just didn't pick up on it. Or saying it to himself. But I caught it. Because I'm here now. Caught it and felt it was significant and personal. I was ready to hear it. Maybe that's the key to all my Visitations."

"Let's take that a little further," Beverly said. "Why would you have felt the words *something I missed* were significant and personal?"

"Well, I hadn't thought about that before. I suppose that finding what's missing has been my mission since I got sick, you know? The fragments of memory, the bits of thought or perception, the words and images. The link between the person I was before getting sick and the person I became. The person I am. So the chance to put some things together is another step toward coherence. 'Something I Missed' should be printed on my T-shirt."

Beverly and I looked at each other in silence for a few moments. "Right," I said. "I should make a note of all this so I don't forget."

When I'd finished, Beverly said, "Back to Hardy and why he was out there. Was he always a lost soul or has he been, I don't know, a lost soul only since he died?"

"Or maybe it started after that book came out, the one about Tryphena and their incestuous family relationships, and Randy. The horror of the rumors." That sounded plausible to me. "When he lost control of his story's dark heart. Could certainly be what he missed—safeguarding his love?"

"Tryphena."

"Or love in general."

As we talked, Beverly typed notes. I watched her fingertips skipping over the keys, becoming mesmerized in my fatigue, and waited till she came to a stop. She looked at me and smiled. "You said there were three mysteries."

"The third is why Hardy is the focus of this kind of attention. And about these kinds of subjects. Some people, many from here in Dorset, seem to need a Hardy who behaved like a rogue, a sexual predator, a scoundrel. Who was like some of the seedy characters in his books. Too full of himself. They want to take him down. And his fervid defenders need him to be pure, the Great Man, though there's ample evidence against that, too. Why turn mild-mannered, timid Thomas Hardy into a Charles Dickens?" I thought about that for a moment and said, "But why not? It was Victorian England and there were few writers who didn't have a scandal attached them. Just took a while to get around to Hardy. All that apparent rectitude in the life, and the shocking transgressions in the work. Hardy's doublings and cover-ups. They couldn't resist. It was blowback. You'd think he'd imagine that something like this would happen no matter what he did to prevent it."

"About those Dorset people, you know, this is the world he came from," Beverly said. "I mean, the world that shaped them shaped him too." Her fingers rested on the keys. "Let's go back for a second to what we said about the Visitation." She checked the screen. "Do you think Hardy was always a lost soul? Or could he be lost now because he could never lose himself when alive?"

"Maybe that's the key. Was he always like that? If not, when did he lose himself?" The next words came out in a whisper. "Was the loss of his love like Hardy's version of my viral attack—the thing that changed him in a flash?"

"Targeting his heart instead of his brain."

≑

We shut down the laptop and left for our walk. My mind felt much clearer, which made me feel less tired, eager to be outside, in the landscape. The day was deep into afternoon, cloudy and cool enough for us to wear hooded jackets. Following Anthony's instructions, we headed over a rolling field toward Hambury Tout and the sea.

In his work, Hardy called "Lulworth" "Lulwind" and "Lulstead." It was a sheltered cove where the sea wind lulled and a ship could rest. But up on the bluffs the wind was fierce enough to convince us we should avoid the hilltop path across the tout and stay tucked on its leeward side. The view was still magnificent, green hills behind, the Jurassic coast ahead, the essential Dorset pastoral scene.

As we neared the sea, though, we encountered a massive crowd of walkers using the famous coastal path, 350 miles down to Land's End. It seemed the half-million annual visitors Anthony had referred to all showed up on the same day. A truck selling Typhoo Tea was parked on the bluff. So many people were speaking so many languages that it overwhelmed the sound of the surf below. We laughed as we waited for enough space to merge into the line.

On the platform above Durdle Door, we stood at the railing that faced west. From there, the view was toward Swyre Head and Weymouth, a dozen miles away. I remembered the scene in *Far from the Madding Crowd* when shepherd Gabriel Oak's sheepdog drives his flock over the cliff right there at Scratchy Bottom. It already seemed natural—unavoidable—to be thinking of the Dorset landscape in terms of Hardy and his work.

Beverly and I took pictures of each other, and asked a fellow walker to take one of the two of us together. Then I took a few steps west until Beverly grabbed my hand and turned me around so we could head toward Lulworth Cove. Hardy had used the cove as the place where his loutish and deceitful Sergeant Troy, also in *Far from the Madding Crowd*, disappeared, swept off in the current. The cove was where smugglers landed illegal brandy in "The Distracted Preacher," where an excursion steamer arrived in *Desperate Remedies*, and most famously where Time whispered in Hardy's ear about the fate of young John Keats, who had stopped there on his short life's final journey toward Italy.

If I'd wanted to stand in Hardy's footsteps, this was another promising location, one he'd come back to at crucial moments in his work. A place of escape by boat or on foot, but also of powerful connection to the literary past he loved.

We paused at the path's high point, where it began its descent into the vast parking lot stretching toward the village from the cove's back. In a gust of wind, I decided to call out Hardy's name. Not so much to summon him, which I didn't believe would work anyway, but just to put it out there, to express my intention to be open and clear as I dug and probed around in his life. To say that I would try to see what was there truly. I understood that Hardy wasn't at my beck and call, and it was possible that I'd never see him again. But still, I felt committed to following through what had begun for me, to find out how the pieces fit.

On the walk downhill, we stayed off the main path to avoid the crowd and the depressing view of the parking lot. We had a clear line of sight to the cove's full arc, carved ten thousand years ago by glacial meltwater. Nearing the bottom, in a meadow barely visible from the shops and restaurants lining the village street, we saw a long wooden table covered with platters of food and pitchers of foamy drink. Two benches along either side of the table were packed with picnickers. Near the table a trio of musicians sat on stools—a burly cellist, two elderly fiddlers swaying as they played—and now I could hear a faint tune within the sounds behind me. A cluster of onlookers stood on a slight rise. I couldn't tell if they were waiting their turns or simply gaping at the noisy, laughing dinner scene.

"Look at what they're all wearing," Beverly said.

I hadn't noticed. Some women wore hooped skirts, others frilly dresses in bright primary colors. Some had bonnets or woolen shawls tied with broad silken ribbons. Bearded men were dressed in rough and well-worn jackets with baggy trousers, some with vests or cravats and high collars. A soldier in full uniform, scarlet and black, stood at the head of the table. One hand clasped his sheathed sword, the other held a mug of beer raised as though he were making a toast. He gestured and beer sloshed onto his wrist, which made him burst into laughter and begin again.

We walked around the edge of the action. The onlookers were also dressed in Victorian costume. No one we could see wore contemporary clothes. I reached for Beverly's hand, steadied by its reality. She was smiling. I tried not to believe we'd gone through a wormhole or a time portal.

One of the fiddlers stopped playing, put down his instrument, and stood. The other musicians stopped then, and everyone watched the fiddler walk toward the table.

"Okay, right," he said. "Very good. Let's take a moment, then start the scene again from where you all say the toast 'To Sergeant Troy and Bathsheba!' But remember, no one's really very happy about this match, all right? Don't be quite so jolly. You know it's not going to end well. *Far from the Madding Crowd*, scene 3. Ready, all?"

8

The next morning we drove to Max Gate, the so-called atmospheric Victorian home designed by Thomas Hardy. It only took half an hour. The first shock was that Max Gate was now part of a sprawling suburban neighborhood girdled by traffic and clusters of young trees, lacking the view and sense of open landscape beyond the walls that I always associated with Hardy's home.

We parked on a weedy border across from the shrub-shrouded red-brick privacy wall. I took a deep breath—the aroma a mingling of blossoms and exhaust—and ran my hand over the entrance post as we walked onto the grounds. A tall man in jeans and baggy sweatshirt was cleaning the lower windows of the conservatory on the building's east side.

Hardy had willed the contents of his Max Gate study to the Dorset County Museum. So now, when you visit Max Gate and look at his study, what you see—the worn, handwoven carpets; the various chairs; the glass-fronted bookcases with their matching vintage volumes; the writing desk with its blank paper, leather blotter, empty wooden manuscript box, pen holder, lamp, magnifying glass, hole punch, framed photograph of Hardy, calendar set forever to the date he and Emma met—is a phantom study. Sure, most writers' houses open to tourists contain facsimile furnishings and knickknacks. But leave it to Hardy to have the real stuff available over there in downtown Dorchester where it had not been during his life, and the fake stuff over here in Max Gate where the real stuff belonged, and where you would look for it. Leave it to Hardy to preserve the real stuff elsewhere, for posterity, while offering the fake stuff at home. Just as in his work, which is where the real Hardy dwelt while the carefully managed façade of Thomas Hardy was offered to the world and to his wife at home. Now you see him, now you don't. All deflection, distraction, smoke and mirrors.

This is the same man whose body's ashes were buried up there in London, in the Poets' Corner of Westminster Abbey, while his heart was buried down here in Dorset's Stinsford Churchyard. Or at least that's the official story handed down since his death in 1928. Because, as with so much else about Hardy, there are rumors about that. Yes, his heart was cut out of his dead body before cremation, and yes, his ashes were then interred in Westminster Abbey. No argument there, and the scenario is certainly weird enough to have come straight from one of Hardy's own later novels. But wait, there's more: his heart was then wrapped in a tea towel and placed inside a biscuit tin for burial in the same grave that housed Emma, the wife he loathed until she died, at which point his love for her erupted in grief and longing and much of the greatest poetry he ever wrote. With attention diverted in the hours after Hardy's death, the undertaker arrived to find the biscuit tin and gory tea towel empty on the kitchen table where the housekeeper had left them. Nearby, Hardy's cat, Cobby, sat licking his stained snout, breath foul with blood's telltale rusty metallic odor. The story would end there if it was about anyone else, but since it's about Hardy, there's a further extreme: the undertaker then killed Cobby, wrapped him in the tea towel with Hardy's heart presumably inside the cat, and put him in the grave. Or the undertaker didn't kill Cobby, but purchased a pig's heart to wrap and bury in the grave. Either way, you still didn't have Hardy's heart where you thought you did.

Just as it wasn't rumor enough that Hardy was in love and had sex with his much-younger cousin Tryphena. The rumor had to metastasize into something nastier: she had to be his niece. Then she had to bear Hardy's child. Anthony and Nan were right: I wouldn't be surprised if a further extreme emerged in regard to Randy, and I heard that Hardy had indeed abandoned the child. Murdered the child. Ate the child.

$$\rightleftharpoons$$

Beverly and I had visited Westminster Abbey and Hardy's ashes nearly a month ago, at the beginning of our trip. We'd decided to spend three days in London, recovering from jet lag and exploring the art galleries, Tate museums, bookstores, landmarks, parks. But the heat and fatigue made us feel like finned snorkelers plodding through endless ankle-high breakers, never able to get far enough for the swimming to begin. We overslept and missed our prepaid breakfast. I lost my balance coming down the stairs of a double-decker bus when the driver braked, and landed in a heap at the bottom. I looked to the right when I should have looked to the left before crossing streets and was nearly splattered by a taxi, asked a waiter if the dressing on our salads was Goodness-free instead of Gluten-free, made a spectacle of myself trying to select the correct coins from my pocket at the Courtauld Gallery. I routinely turned in the wrong direction leaving our hotel, only to feel Beverly's hand find me and set me aright. In St. James Park, where we went to see the pelicans, mute swans, coots, and greenfinch, I massaged Beverly's feet as we sat on the grass in the Queens' backyard, a simple act that would have been scandalous in Hardy's day. At Parliament Square, raucous strikers protesting a tax on recycling had parked their trucks and were blaring horns, the sound an aptly cacophonous accompaniment to the way we felt.

It was midafternoon of the third day by the time we got to Westminster Abbey. Guided by the voice of Jeremy Irons, I tried to pay attention to details of Henry VII's Lady Chapel and Sir Edward the Confessor's Shrine, statues of the saints, but was too impatient to reach Poet's Corner. When we entered it, we shut the audio tour off and simply stood there. At first, my attention was held by footsteps and whispers and the hushed, disembodied sound of Jeremy Irons seeping from other visitors' headphones. A large rose window provided the room's light. In the marble floor there were engraved slabs or memorial markers, the names and sometimes the remains of writers whose work I had read aloud onto tape all those years ago: Browning, Tennyson, Hopkins, Byron. There were busts of Southey, Burns, Drayton; a statue of Shakespeare holding a manuscript in his hand while leaning against a stack of books, another of a demurely down-looking Jane Austen seated in a chair.

Hardy's ashes were immediately to the north of Charles Dickens and the east of Rudyard Kipling. Dickens's marker was larger than theirs combined. I stood before Hardy's name, looking down, and found myself thinking about the story of Hardy taking Kipling on an autumn bicycle excursion to Weymouth for a few days as the younger man searched for a house to buy. At one they inspected, the elderly occupant hadn't heard of her famous visitors and wasn't sure she believed their claims. Now here they are.

Glancing around, I noticed that Hardy was buried in an area of the room otherwise devoted to great actors (Laurence Olivier, Henry Irving, Peggy Ashcroft, and David Garrick), to writers who were extravagant performers of Self (Charles Dickens, Samuel Johnson, and Rudyard Kipling), or to artists who did their enduring work for performance (playwrights Richard Brinsley Sheridan and Richard Cumberland, and composer George Frideric Handel).

This struck me then as a bizarre placement. Reticent, remote Thomas Hardy alone among nine artists of show, nine towering players or creators of roles? But it strikes me, now that I've come to know more about Hardy's life, as stunningly appropriate. Hardy fabricated an understated persona, quiet and reserved, detached and settled, a man who wrote of emotional turbulence while living an outwardly calm life of probity and order, and sold it the way a great actor would. He created a space around his unruly Self into which the attention of others was meant to flow. Hardy's performance seemed part of his nature, the way a killdeer is programmed to perform a broken-wing display in order to distract those who come too near its nest.

Max Gate wasn't as ghastly and inhospitable as I'd expected. From the edge of its horseshoe-shaped driveway, I imagined a flickering overlay of photos taken from right there: Hardy at fifty reading his mail in the garden while his dog, Moss, gazes up at him; Hardy at sixty standing beside his bicycle; Hardy in his seventies with Florence and their dog, Wessex—faithful, unflinching—famous for biting notable literary guests; Hardy in his eighties on the porch with his friend Edmund Gosse; Hardy wizened and wispy by a hedge in the weeks before his death.

This building had been sneered at for 127 years. It had been called oddly uninviting, mean and pretentious, cheerless, a brick mediocrity with no grace of design or detail, a building lacking conventional architectural distinction and proportion, deficient alike in aesthetic qualities and domestic arrangements, the solidification in brick of Hardy's intermittent mood of helplessness at the ugliness of life. Having read all that, and seen dozens of images, I was braced for the building's inelegance and asymmetry, its heavy presence. But being there in person, I felt Max Gate was consistent with Hardy's patterns as I was beginning to understand them: a bland, even off-putting exterior that deflected interest, that covered up and contradicted the life roiling inside. It was architectural disinformation, a front. I felt the force of his intentions everywhere around there, his resolve to be seen but not *seen*. To erect another space around his Self into which the attention of others was meant to flow.

I posed beside the front door with the Max Gate sign above my left shoulder, where I'd first felt Hardy's presence on South Street. I was dressed in shades of gray—clothes, hair, beard—and the wall behind me was splotched with gray so that I seemed to fade into the building, to or take shape from within it like a developing image on film.

Max Gate was built by Hardy's father and brother according to plans developed by Hardy himself. We'd noticed his smudged sectional drawings yesterday at the Dorset County Museum. This was a project that would combine all that mattered most to him: shaping a place to accommodate and support his writing, contain his marriage, satisfy his need for privacy and solitude, express his assertion that he belonged. It was all that he meant by Home. Meticulous, always concerned about nuance, Hardy first placed the house so it faced his childhood home at Higher Bockhampton some three miles northeast. Then he turned the design around so it faced south and away from the past. There aren't even windows looking back.

He named it Max Gate in tribute to Henry Mack, who'd once managed a toll gate nearby. Mack's Gate became Max Gate, which acknowledged Mack but, by removing the apostrophe, clarified that he was not the owner of the place, a simultaneous and typically Hardyean nod to tradition and change in one gesture. For me, Hardy's rechristening of Mack's to Max highlighted another intimate coincidence between us. Max was the name my crusty maternal grandfather Markus took when rechristening himself upon arrival in America, and it's the name Beverly and I chose to rechristen our tabby cat, who'd been named Rufus when we adopted him from the Willamette Humane Society.

Work on Max Gate went slowly. The Hardys did most of it themselves, with few laborers onsite at any time. Materials came from the family brickyard at Broadmayne. Hardy planted thousands of beeches and Austrian pines as a windbreak and shield against onlookers. There was contentiousness on the job, an undercurrent of tension as Hardy's aged father offered advice, Hardy's brother had other priorities, costs intensified, and Emma complained about having to settle in Dorset instead of London. It took nineteen months before Hardy and Emma could occupy the house in June 1885, three years before part of the drawing-room ceiling collapsed, ten years before he swore off writing novels and turned to poetry, fourteen years before Emma moved upstairs to live in the attic.

"Whether building this house at Max Gate was a wise expenditure of energy is one doubt, which, if resolved in the negative, is depressing enough," Hardy wrote.

Sir Nikolaus Pevsner, a British scholar of the history of architecture, offset his scathing judgment about the building—"Unfortunately the house has no architectural qualities whatever"—by acknowledging that the environs speak more eloquently of Hardy's personality than the house itself. That's something I felt as soon as I entered the grounds. The environs were all about gardens and the flow of light; about being enveloped by nature, as in the long, narrow tree-enclosed zone called the Nut Walk, perfect both for hiding and contemplative isolation; about having room to lavish attention on his pets whether living or dead.

Everything about Max Gate forced a visitor to face the fact that Hardy was an architect. In fact, he had far more serious training as an architect than as a writer, apprenticing to a Dorchester architect at sixteen, working around Dorset and Cornwall as well as in London, where he won prizes from the Royal Institute of British Architects and the Architectural Association, continuing to practice until the age of thirty-two. Whether he was a good architect, or rather whether he was a suitable one to design warm, intimate spaces conducive to love, is beside the point. Max Gate was his architectural brainchild, and he approached the building of his home as he approached his writing and his life and ultimately his legacy: as things to be neatly, precisely designed and shaped by himself. Each detail had purpose. In the study's windows there were no mullions or transoms to block his garden view. The living room windows and corresponding dining room windows were at different heights because in one he wanted to allow a view out and in the other he wanted to block the view in. He made sure the house had rooms for him to work and hide in, a secret door for him to escape from visitors and vanish into the trees. In time, his wife withdrew from the living areas. The place could hardly have been more his, which in part explains why Emma ended up in the attic.

≈

Without guests on the grounds, and with the window cleaner gone into the house, I could sense the ghostly presence of the past everywhere. Max Gate had always been like that. In 1883, when the site was being prepared and foundations dug, Romano-British skeletal remains, urns, and relics were unearthed. The bodies had each been folded into oval holes in the chalk like chicks in their eggshells. Though he and Emma thought the omens might be gloomy, Hardy took a pair of Iron Age brooches from one skeleton's forehead, and turned a huge sandstone block found atop another skeleton into a Druid stone tucked into his garden hedge. There was a ring-neck flask from the time of Emperor Claudius. Hardy read an account of his findings at a meeting of the Dorset Field Club in 1884. Through the years, pottery and tableware kept being discovered in the garden and stored in Hardy's study, where he mined the past for stories, poems, and drama.

This feeling of being awash in the past, of being loose in Time again, made me think of the conversation we'd had with Anthony over breakfast that morning. He'd brought plates of fruits and yogurt, a pot of tea, asked how we wanted our eggs prepared. But instead of returning to the kitchen, he pulled over a chair from the adjacent table.

"You don't mind if I sit for a moment?"

"We'd like that," Beverly said.

I'd reached for the teapot, but hesitated, not sure if I should continue. Anthony poured, passed the milk.

"Nan and I were talking about what happened to you yesterday in Dorchester. I hope my response didn't seem inhospitable. Believe me, I had no intention to be flippant about what you experienced."

"I didn't take it that way, Anthony." Where was this was going to lead? "And I know what I said must have sounded very strange."

Anthony was looking away as if unwilling to speak too directly at me. "Not to me. Not at all, actually, and last night Nan reminded me of something. This goes back to 1982. Falkland Islands." He paused and let his eyes meet mine long enough to determine if I knew what he was referring to. "I was part of the invasion task force, you see. Aboard the *Hermes*. It was April, spring here but autumn in the South Atlantic. Topsy-turvy, and when you're out there at sea, at war, you can lose track a bit. Time of day, time of year, where you are. Lose touch. I'm going on a bit, sorry."

We both urged him to continue. I still didn't get how this was tied to my having been Visited by Hardy, and I hoped Anthony didn't think I was just disoriented and in need of care.

"Well, then. This one night—it was three in the morning—I woke up and understood myself to have entered some sort of fold or rift in time. Or outside of time. I've tried to explain it for thirty years. Sir Francis Drake, Jack Hawkins, Charles Darwin, Percy Fawcett, all around me were people who had sailed those waters throughout history. There were my mates aboard, too, clear as stone. And also faces I felt sure were from the time to come, as if I were remembering the future. I was awake, I was of sound mind. But I was what you might call 'between dimensions.' Time stopped dead. For a moment, over—or I should say within—the engine's thrumming and the sound of moving air I either heard or imagined, there was a voice. Whose voice I do not know."

Anthony drew himself up in his chair, where he'd slumped as he spoke. He stiffened his back and stretched, determined to continue.

"The voice spoke to me the words *Call him Hermes* as unmistakably as Thomas Hardy spoke to you the words *Something I missed*."

I could hardly breathe. I had to fight against an impulse to embrace him.

"That was the name of the ship you were on," Beverly said.

Anthony nodded. "Her Majesty's Ship, the *Hermes*. Named after the Greek god of transitions and boundaries."

"I'd forgotten that," I said.

"So had I, till one of the Royal Navy pilots reminded me. Transitions and boundaries. Quite astounding."

"Did you know what that voice in the night meant?" Beverly asked.

"Not then. But in a letter a few weeks later, Nan told me she was pregnant." He pointed to a photo on the wall near the kitchen door. "That young man in uniform? That's our son, Hermes. Hermes Christopher Evans Swain. Goes by Herm."

We all looked across at the photo in silence. Herm looked so much like the photos of his father in uniform scattered around the B&B, I was sure I'd walked by a few and thought they were Anthony.

"So you did what it told you to do," I said.

Anthony rubbed one of his large hands over his freshly shaven face and sighed. "We lost 255 British during those seventy-four days of the war. Including my cousin and dearest friend, Christopher Evans."

Oh. Anthony looked at me, then at Beverly, then stood up. "There are voices one must listen to, aren't there?" He smiled. "I'll deal with your eggs now."

All I could do was stir my tea. He—and Nan—had given us a generous and intimate gift in sharing this story, and I felt grateful for the implicit acceptance of my own experience. Also, subtly encouraged to continue following after Hardy and his voice. Anthony had heeded a message he'd received in the same way I'd received mine, though it must have caused him pain not to name his son directly for the cousin he'd lost.

Now, walking down the driveway to the front door of Max Gate, I thought again of Anthony's face in the moment he'd spoken the name Hermes Christopher Evans Swain. I realized what it recalled: a photo of Hardy's wife Emma Gifford Hardy in her fifties, but looking older. She is facing the camera squarely in a way she seldom did, hair parted and pulled back flat against her head rather than stacked and curling as customary for her. She isn't smiling. There is nothing childlike or innocent here, nothing pretentious or haughty either, as in so many other images of Emma. This is a person stripped of artifice and carrying an intense hurt, a person who reckons all that has been lost and—for just this moment—lets us see her pain, her sadness, and her strength.

9

There was an unopened guest book on a table in Max Gate's entrance hall. A pen dangled from it on a gold chain, stirred by our arrival, catching meager lamplight. The space was small and cold, filled with the ticking of grandfather clocks coming from the dining room, drawing room, beside the staircase, and somewhere back behind it as well. It seemed right only to whisper there.

I leaned close to Beverly. "God, it's eerie."

"And dark, even with the door open."

The staircase, now that I looked more closely, appeared wide for such a modest nook, designed in the old manner to accommodate a loaded coffin coming down. The stairwell wall was lined with framed maps and Dorset landscapes, a few faded faces, illustrations from several of Hardy's novels.

We heard footsteps above. A throat-clearing cough. Then the man I'd seen cleaning windows peeked around the corner of the landing, his hair wet.

"Just changing clothes. Down in a few moments. Why don't you have a look around the drawing room there and I'll be right with you." He waved and withdrew, then returned. "I'm Jason, by the way. Jason Abbott. The third. Max Gate's caretaker this year." He waved again, then added, "I mean, you can sit in there, if you wish. Not only look around. In the drawing room. Oh, and forgive the stuffed terrier by the fireplace. Won't bite. Sorry. Just a bit of Hardy humor."

"Then his name mustn't be Wessex," I said.

"Hah! You know your Hardy trivia." With that, and without waving, he vanished and we heard him tromping back upstairs.

The ticking hush returned, and the chilliness. I took a National Trust / Max Gate pamphlet from a stack beside the guestbook, and glanced at the floor plan on its back page. It showed that besides the dining and drawing rooms, the only rooms available to the public were two of Hardy's first-floor studies, and two attic rooms—one belonging to Emma and the other to her young maid, Dolly Gale. It felt quite right to be only somewhat welcome to but a part of Hardy's home.

I was learning that even as he invited you in, Hardy eluded you. He was certainly doing that with me, having been in contact twice but vanishing behind the riddle of his message and the illusion of his presence. And the various Hardy tourist sites, as operated by the National Trust and local volunteers, appear to have caught that spirit, the mixture of exposure and circumspection, balancing the demand for access with the need for guardedness.

We tiptoed into the dining room. Its linen-covered table was topped with two silver tea trays, an empty vase, a pair of unused red candles. I tried not to focus on what was missing—the cups, spoons, dishes, napkins, water glasses. An arrangement of purple irises and ferns filled the open hearth. According to the pamphlet, there was some of Hardy's own furniture in the room, on loan from the Dorset County Museum. So that was his actual bookcase bureau, his scroll arm sofa, his chairs at the table's ends. There were no obvious cobwebs or dust, but the impression was of long absence, not anticipation. Of life stopped, not paused. A vague memory of what families and friends did together. It was hard to imagine eating in this room, laughing, being relaxed and natural, open to intimacy. The rug with its deep purples and wines reminded me of one in my daughter's Chicago home, and I tried to focus on that, to connect with the warmth or coziness that can come with dining together. But it was no use.

We turned around and recrossed the hall to stand just inside the drawing room. What met my eyes was visual mayhem. For a re-created Victorian-era villa's drawing room, I'm sure it was accurate, a typical homey, charmingly busy space. But for me, so easily confused by visual stimuli in the wake of neurological damage, the effect was overwhelming. What I saw was all clashing colors and shapes, arm chairs and easy chairs and desk chairs, a tumult of decorative touches and optical distractions. Available surfaces were covered with plates, baskets, figurines, odd pieces of pottery and metal. The glass-fronted bookcase and mirror over the fireplace threw back a clamor of images and light.

Where was Hardy in all this? Near the room's center was an oval table draped in a violet cloth on which a half-dozen photographs clustered. I tried to concentrate on them. Even from the entryway I could recognize the pointy-bearded portrait of the balding author in his midforties that had been on the cover of the first Hardy biography I'd read. There was an aging Emma beside him, there was Florence, his parents, everyone facing different directions. Yellow English roses drooped from a vase and covered half of another photograph. The stuffed terrier lay on its side before the empty fireplace. By the window, a group of chairs and footstools was covered in upholstery so profusely flowered that I wanted to move them away from the light to stop their spread.

I knew from images I'd seen in books that the Max Gate drawing room had been cluttered. But those images had been in fuzzy black and white and this was living color and we were right there. I felt a wash of tenderness for Emma. To me, the room seemed to express her nearly un-manageable energies, trapped as they were by her marriage, by living in Max Gate, in Dorset.

What came to mind—again with the Yiddish—was the word *tchotchkes*, which refers to trinkets and baubles but also means *bruise*. You could, and I often did as a child because of my mother's explosive rages, have a little tchotchke under your eye, the word implying that the mark was slight, was nothing, a trifle not to be spoken of, though the person bearing the tchotchke knew differently. The close link between the two—the jumble of stuff in Max Gate's most public space as a homonym for the sort of small bruises that mark our passage—struck me powerfully as I tried to sort out what I was seeing.

The drawing room was both physically and metaphorically the dining room's opposite, loud instead of quiet, immoderate instead of austere. I don't know what I expected to feel in visiting Max Gate, but it wasn't this increasing sense of intense sadness. The deeper I found myself in Hardy's private world, the longer I dwelt in it, the clearer I saw confusion, regret, and pain. Saw fragmentation rather than coherence.

In the drawing room, he and Emma—and later, he and Florence—hosted the great figures of literary life in Victorian England, the people among whom Hardy had earned his place. Here they chatted with Robert Louis Stevenson, H. G. Wells, Virginia Woolf, T. E. Lawrence, George Bernard Shaw. Here was where Wessex nipped John Galsworthy's leg and Emma talked with W. B. Yeats about her cat and Hardy met Charles Dickens's last surviving son, where honors were bestowed on Hardy and performances of his work were given and parties spilled out over the lawn. It was the one place above all where Hardy saw the dimensions of his achievement made manifest. But it didn't look like a place where he'd be comfortable or at ease, where he'd smile.

He was to be found, I thought, somewhere between the dining room's impassivity and the drawing room's turbulence. Maybe he was in the vestibule's hushed ticking.

"What are you thinking?" Beverly whispered.

"That I can sense the bitterness here."

It was like an odor that couldn't be covered over by any cleansing agent, a stain that couldn't be hidden by any number of diverting whatnots, a bruise spreading rather than being contained by time and the process of healing. It was all of that at once, a disruption of atmosphere.

⇒

The chandelier didn't rattle, but there was no mistaking the sound of Jason storming back downstairs. We heard him stop on the landing as though gathering himself, then take the final flight down more lightly. He opened the guest book and placed the pen beside it before joining us.

"Right. Sorry. Wasn't quite ready. Official welcome." He shook our hands. Then he took hand sanitizer from his pocket, squirted a dab in his palm, and passed the container to us. "Can't be too careful, I say. So, a Hardy scholar?"

I shook my head. "Just a longtime reader. Also written about him a few times, trying to figure out what I think."

"Ahhh. Very good." Jason seemed relieved that I wasn't a scholar. "And what do you think?"

"That keeps changing."

"Of course." Jason used more hand sanitizer, since Beverly and I had touched the container, then repocketed it. He turned toward Beverly and said, "That's the most exciting reading, isn't it? When you haven't made up your mind."

"Well, there's something to be said for reading a writer you know you love, too."

It was clear that Jason hadn't been expecting an actual, thoughtful response. He blinked several times—a Hugh Grant moment—before saying "Quite right, quite right. Who would that be for you?"

Beverly closed her eyes. "These days I'm into novels by contemporary women." She kept her eyes closed, taking silent inventory. "I always love Ann Patchett's work and look forward to the next one. Barbara Kingsolver. Pam Houston. In the UK there's Maggie O'Farrell, Hilary Mantel, Helen Simonson. Just discovered Claire Morrall."

As she was speaking, Jason plucked a notebook and pen from another pocket and wrote frantically. "Great! Will text this list to my girlfriend. In Dublin until autumn. Desperate for good novels by women."

"Tell her Jennifer Johnston and Deirdre Madden, then."

"Wait. What am I doing?" He stopped writing. "Ex-girlfriend. Separation, my idea, no contact until the end of September." He shrugged and repocketed his notebook and pen. "That's part of it, you see. Everything between us had become habit."

"Were you together a long time?"

"Seemed like it, at the end." Then he squared his shoulders and said, "Sorry. So shall I give you the speech?" He assumed a robot voice, cocked his head, spread his arms, and recited, "Max Gate was built on one and a half acres Thomas Hardy purchased from the Duchy of Cornwall. Max Gate was designed by Thomas Hardy. Max Gate was where Thomas Hardy wrote the following books . . ."

"No, that's all right. We'll just rout the rest of the house."

Jason blinked at me. "You'll what?"

"He means *tour*," Beverly said. "We'll just tour the rest of the house."

Jason studied me for a moment, as though concerned I'd just revealed my intention to damage Max Gate.

"I have some neurological issues," I told him. "Some word-finding problems. Sorry."

"No problem. Fascinating, actually. Right then, you'll tour the house. Happy to escort you. Until others arrive, anyway." He took a step toward the dining room, then stopped. "Oops. Been there, done that, right? Upstairs we go."

As we approached the staircase, Beverly asked Jason how long he'd been working at Max Gate. He didn't answer till we'd reached the landing.

"Actually, I'm in residence here. Two years. Technically, tenant slash caretaker slash scholar-in-residence. Began March the first."

"I didn't know there was such a program," I said.

"I'm the second one. Before me, a woman came over from America. Wrote her dissertation, kept the place up, got Hardy's studies ready for public display."

"What are you working on?"

Jason began walking up the remaining stairs. "Don't like to talk about it, you see. Jinx." He looked back over his shoulder. "Well, not so much a jinx. You know, so many people come to Max Gate for research. Don't want to accidentally give someone ideas, right?"

"I understand." Clearly, the notion of scholarly competition made him edgy.

But he couldn't help himself. The desire to reveal what he'd dedicated himself to study was as strong as the desire to conceal its secrets. He stopped as we reached the first floor and spoke to the wall ahead rather than to us.

"Say this much: its title is *Love's Geometry: The Coordinates of Relationship in the Novels of Thomas Hardy*. Although this morning whilst cleaning the conservatory windows I thought perhaps the subtitle should be *Measuring Love in the Novels of Thomas Hardy* instead. Or maybe *Formulas for Love*." He shrugged and pointed toward the rooms that were closed off. "That's my part of the house. Study and bedroom." He motioned behind us. "Over there, Hardy's second study and beyond that his final study. We can go in."

But he didn't budge, so neither did we. He was moving his lips as though arguing with himself, and losing the struggle to hide his ideas for the subject of his book. "One more thing. Since you asked. My view, the central drama in the novels is always a character trying to choose among two or three or even four potential loves. Hence love's geometry."

He looked at me, perhaps to see if I agreed. Or was taking stealthy notes. I said, "The Tess-Angel-Alec triangle."

"Exactly. Hardy was working like that quite early. Does the heroine pick the rustic musician, the wealthy farm owner, or the stodgy Parson? Next book: does the heroine pick the small-town architect, the big-city book reviewer, or the wealthy local lord? Next book: does she pick the sturdy shepherd, the wealthy farmer, or the dashing soldier? Next book: the returning native with education and character, or the wild innkeeper? Next book: the heir to the estate, the sailor, or his brother the trumpet-major? And so on, for fourteen books."

Thus far, Jason hadn't revealed anything casual readers of Hardy's novels wouldn't have recognized on their own. The basic Hardy plot. I thought, He's pulling a Hardy. He's confiding without disclosing. Beverly was motionless and watching Jason closely, reading him, and I could sense her disciplined patience. Okay, she's right, I need to give him time.

"I'm interested in the forces that made Hardy obsess about having to choose among competing lovers. Did that even before it became a reality in his own life. Or to put it differently, what made him obsess about how rare it is to find all one yearns for in a single person? So that choosing *this* love means losing *that* love. Never getting it all. Missing out."

"And the solution is never found."

"No, the solution is never found. He just stops looking." Jason turned his head toward Hardy's final study. "In 1895, after *Jude the Obscure* was published and savaged by the reviewers, Hardy quit writing novels."

"And you think that's why he quit? He gave up trying to solve the problem, or work out the angles, or whatever?"

Jason seemed to nod, but I wasn't sure he'd even heard me. In fact, I wasn't sure I'd spoken aloud. I was trying to keep up with him, but felt myself starting to drift away at the same time.

"The geometry of love," Jason had said. Twice. It was a phrase that brought me back to my mentor, Robert Russell, who had died just a year ago, at the age of eighty-six. We'd kept in touch over the years since I graduated, and I'd last seen him five years earlier, when I returned to Franklin and Marshall to receive an honorary degree at their 2006 commencement exercises. Being with him then had spurred me to re-read Hardy when I got back home. I would phone Russell to talk about my reading, and then wrote an essay—dedicated to him—about the way he and Hardy had helped give shape to my life.

*

Russell's high-pitched voice told me the same thing it told me nearly forty years before: "Thomas Hardy is not a good writer." Knowing what came next, I nodded, though he couldn't see me. "But he is a great writer."

I had him on speakerphone so I could keep both hands free to take notes. I swear I smelled his pipe, saw ashes on his clothing, papers scattered around his desk. His hair flared wildly on the sides, where it was white, and rose to a neat black mound on top, like Egdon Heath. Brows twitched, smile widened, hands settled after brief flight. Only his closed eyes seemed still.

"It's Hardy's struggle to speak, that's what matters. To say what he's trying to say. Not the accomplishment, but the struggle."

"I remember you telling me that when I was working on my thesis, and I didn't fully understand what you meant."

"Mmmm. But you do now, don't you?"

As he so often had done, Russell was saying several things at once, and saying it by asking a question I didn't need to answer. He was acknowledging my illness and the way it forced me to evolve a new way of writing, of speaking. But he was also acknowledging the effect of time and experience and love on my ability to understand what was less apparent to me as a student. He was referring to my rereading of Hardy at the time we spoke. And he was, metaphorically, embracing me while also setting me free, suggesting that I might not need his mentorship any longer. I knew, though, that I still needed him.

He'd been Dr. Russell to me throughout my college years. I just couldn't call him Bob, though I called my other professors by their given names. In my thoughts and when I wrote about him, he was Russell. I'd managed a mumbled Bob earlier in this conversation, since he'd insisted, but now that we were talking about Hardy there was no way I could Bob him. So I skipped the name business and answered his question. Did I understand what he meant by the importance of the struggle to speak. "Nearly, I think."

"I remember the hard time you had with *The Trumpet-Major*," Russell said, his voice soaring with amusement. "When you said you didn't want to finish it, I suggested that you add *The Dynasts* to your reading list instead."

I remembered that too. The thought had terrified me as I sat beside him, midway through my project. Once I'd learned of its existence, I dreaded having to plough through Hardy's three-part poetic epic drama about the Napoleonic Wars: 662 pages! 297 speaking parts! "Why didn't you assign it anyway?"

He chuckled. "Oh my, then you'd have had to read it to me, wouldn't you?"

Russell's voice was so deeply lodged in my memory that its sound survives all the brain damage that ensued, and often returns in dreams. I loved how expressive its tones were, the melody of his speech, and the way his language was peppered with Britishisms from his years living in England.

As I listened to him then, I was in two places at once, separated by nearly forty years. And I realized that at the time I'd begun reading the novels, Hardy had been dead for only forty years. Such a brief time. Forty years was only as long as Carson McCullers had been dead at the time we spoke, or Langston Hughes, or Dorothy Parker. Yet those writers seemed much closer to me than Hardy had seemed in 1968, contemporary in ways Hardy never could, even if he'd still been alive when I was reading him.

Part of the reason was that he wrote his fourteen published novels during the quarter century between 1870 and 1895. So while he lived until 1928, those novels were more distant, the work of the middle third of his life, when he was between thirty and fifty-five. But even young, Hardy had an old man's grumpy, bitter outlook, and he wasn't writing about a world I recognized as a twenty-year-old.

Yet for all his remoteness from life as I knew it, there was something about Hardy's sensibility, a long-standing, childhood-borne feeling of gloom and radical dislocation, a yearning sadness, that resonated across the years. I felt drawn to Hardy, and still do. There was a core of long-standing deep pain in him, the pain of a rejected child, a child unable to express his deepest feelings and needs. I also associated Hardy's pain with despondency over love. The novels are all driven by a crazed vision of love as torment. It was a vision I recognized viscerally, having witnessed my parents' mutual harrowing, their volatile misery. When Hardy wrote of Eustacia Vye, in *The Return of the Native*, that "the only way to look queenly without realms or hearts to queen it over is to look as if you had lost them," he could have been describing my mother on any given day. At the Russian Tea Room, for instance, presenting herself as an aristocrat and abusing the servants. When Michael Henchard, in *The Mayor of Casterbridge*, sold his wife to the highest bidder and hoped never to see her again, he was living out my father's deepest wish. When Henchard dies a lonely death at the novel's end, a clear failure to thrive in the wake of his lovelorn misery, it resonated with my unhappy father's death by drowning while having a heart attack with no one around to save him. I found my parents' enormous disappointment, thwarted ambitions, and explosive unhappiness enacted throughout Hardy's work. I also found my own inheritance of pain and loss, the urgency to understand what love could be, how it might survive our wounds.

My mother often talked about having chosen the wrong man from among her many suitors. A one-eyed chicken butcher when she could have married a doctor lawyer composer actor billionaire baron earl prince. As Jason Abbott III said to me and Beverly on the first floor of Max Gate, this sort of romantic dilemma was everywhere in Hardy's novels. Love's geometry. And in the rare cases when characters did end up in a tolerable union, it was by settling, as Bathsheba Everdene did with Gabriel Oak at the end of *Far from the Madding Crowd*, for "good fellowship—camaraderie," which Hardy called "the only love which is as strong as death—that love which many waters cannot quench, nor the floods drown, beside which the passion usually called by the name is evanescent as steam."

I didn't believe Hardy believed that claptrap about camaraderie being better than passion, not deep down in his soul. His characters yearned for—needed—the passion that inevitably ravaged their lives. It seemed to be what made them come alive. Characters accidentally touched hands in a basin of water and were overwhelmed by desire. Characters bedazzled one another with sudden gentleness, or with displays of manly brio or feminine bravado. On passion's flip side, a spurned lover cut off and sold her gorgeous locks of hair. Another discovered that the wife who abandoned him had financed her escape by selling his framed wedding portrait. Hardy was at his best in moments of love's urgency or agony, its intimate wounding.

I felt that I knew what Hardy was struggling to say in these extraordinary scenes, his heat and heartbreak evident in the rare imagistic eloquence of his prose, the ardor of the writing. I also felt that I grasped what underlay his sense of love's geometry, and how we sometimes cannot want or desire what is good for us, how rare it is when the angles all balance. How ideals—theorems—are useless in the realities of love as it happens in the world.

I remembered one meeting with Russell, sometime in early 1969, when we were discussing Tess's sad fate, her abuse at the hands of Alec D'Urberville, her abandonment by Angel Clare. I tried to explain how much the novel disappointed me, with its heavy-handed heaping of debasement on Tess, but yet how powerfully it moved me. I knew from the way my parents acted toward each other and toward me that there might be no limit to what people do to those they love. The novel's climactic scene at Stonehenge, so redolent of human sacrifice, particularly galled me even as it touched and terrified me. As a child I'd had dreams of being sacrificed, like Isaac bound on the altar, in just such a place. I stammered, and though he couldn't see my eyes filling with tears Russell understood what was happening.

"This is it, you know," he said. "This is the struggle to say what you're trying to say."

It's the sort of thing some fathers say to their sons at such moments. I think I knew then, as our time together neared its end, that Russell had become much more than an employer or professor or even a mentor to me. He had led me to find my voice, to speak as myself. He had also led me to Thomas Hardy, helping me understand that Hardy was an example of struggling to speak the heart.

I couldn't call him Bob, and I didn't want to call him Bob, for the same reasons I could never have called my father Harry. But it didn't occur to me until forty years later, hearing him talk again about Hardy's struggle to speak, but also alluding to my own struggles in the aftermath of my illness and to all I'd learned since being his student (Mmmm. But you do now, don't you?), that if he'd suggested we study Arnold or Browning or Carlyle or Hopkins or Tennyson I would have agreed. But he'd suggested Hardy, said, "I have a feeling for Hardy, and I think you might too." It was as though he'd known exactly who and what I needed. Then, and in the future.

As our phone call neared its end, Russell said he'd enjoyed seeing me again when I was back on campus. I always loved how he'd used the verb *see* without self-consciousness, freeing people to speak more easily to him as well. I told him it had been good to see him too, that he'd looked well, had hardly changed at all.

"That's what I think when I look in the mirror too," he said.

"When I'm done with this essay on Hardy, I'll make a recording and send it to you."

"I'll look forward to that. And meanwhile, tell Beverly again how glad I was to meet her, finally. I can see that you're both happy together."

I don't know why I said what I said next, but am glad I did. "What do you think Hardy would have made of it?"

"Oh, he'll tell you eventually."

10

Late-morning light engulfed a writing desk by the east-facing window in Hardy's study. It also blanched a pair of worn rugs in the middle of the room, ricocheted off the glass-fronted bookcase at the far wall, pooled on the polished surface of a small table in the corner. Hardy had achieved radiant overkill in the design of this space. There was no need for them, but the desk lamps and ceiling fixture were lit too. Looking at it as I had earlier, from outside—and knowing the gloominess of spirit shadowing Max Gate—I hadn't imagined a study space anywhere near so bright. Hardy could work in this? Perhaps it let him see more deeply into his own darkness.

The desk held scattered piles of manuscript papers. I knew they couldn't be Hardy's, but walked over to examine them and found dozens of poems, drawings, and notes from recent visitors to Max Gate. "You will not be disappointed," someone had written. Another had scrawled the name Thomas Hardy over and over, the signature diminishing in size as it neared the bottom of the page, where it stopped in midname: Thomas Ha. A child had drawn the lopsided outline of a house with three stick figures towering over it and the sun in five different locations. In purple ink and deft calligraphy, there were lines from Hardy's poem "Old Furniture": "I see the hands of the generations / That owned each shiny familiar thing."

I sat in the desk chair. My absurd impulse was to tidy the writing surface, smooth out the blotter, align the glue pot with the pen box. And draw the blinds. But this was supposed to be his space, not mine. Except we all knew it was only the illusion of Hardy's space. It smelled like wall paint and furniture polish.

What is it, I wondered, that drives us to pursue writers beyond the boundaries of their books? Why do we need more from them than they give us there? Hardy certainly despised this pursuit: "I think," he wrote to a journalist in 1906, "that to get behind a book at the author of a book, who has naturally said in his own pages all that we wants to say, is a vicious custom which ought to be discontinued."

How does sitting at a desk that was not Hardy's real desk and picking up a pen that was not his pen and even writing his own words there on paper that was not his paper bring us closer to the writer whose words fill our minds? Apparently the writer's words alone are not sufficient, but seeing or touching the relics of a life might be. As though this brings us closer to the place where the life and the art alchemize.

Of course, I was guilty of doing it myself. I'm a reader who loves literary biography, loves visiting the homes of writers I admire, touching up against their lives. Earlier on this trip to England, I'd visited Dylan Thomas's Boat House home at Laugharne, in southwestern Wales, peered into his writing shed, sat on his terrace, saw the river and harbor below, the green hills, the seabirds, watched a video in his upstairs bedroom. I spent time walking where John Fowles had walked in Lyme Regis, stood on the windy Cobb where the French Lieutenant's woman stood, and hiked in the Undercliff by the sea where so much had happened in Fowles's novel. A few years ago, when my daughter was living in Memphis and had just finished writing her book, we drove down to Oxford, Mississippi, and visited William Faulkner's white clapboard home, Rowan Oak, walking together through a line of cedars toward its shadowy portico. As her own office wall had been, Faulkner's was covered with notes charting his book's structure. We leaned side-by-side over the threshold.

As I writer, I'm wary of this curiosity in others. As a father, too, since people assume an artificial intimacy with my daughter based on her work, feeling at liberty to reach out to her because in her book she is so approachable, so warm. But as a reader, I love giving in to it.

Feeling drowsy in the sun's warmth, gazing out the window toward Hardy's garden, I thought about things I possessed that might be of interest to people who knew my work. I couldn't come up with much: This was Floyd's recliner, where he spent so much time during the first years of his illness. Notice the melted patches where it got too close to the wood-burning stove. And this is the Brooklyn Dodgers baseball hat he used to wear when he wrote in the morning. Later, after his daughter moved to Chicago, he began wearing the Chicago Cubs hat you see on the bookshelf. That photo is Floyd and Beverly on their wedding day. Notice how their round house looks dwarfed by all those second-growth oak?

And what would I want to hide? What was I hiding while writing four memoirs that were intended to let me reassemble myself from fragments of the past, the shards of my story that were left in a shattered memory system? I believed I was on an essential journey of discovery and had to see the fullest truth or else I myself would be transformed into a lie. I was desperate not to hide anything, but can I be sure I succeeded? Am I hiding something now, even something I'm not aware of hiding?

I heard Beverly laugh behind me, and turned to see her standing in the doorway with a cat in her arms. It was Bella, Jason told us, a stalwart mouser named after Arabella Donn in *Jude the Obscure*. I stood, realizing how close I'd been to falling asleep, and in the comfort of hearing Beverly's delight mingling with Bella's, I felt a sense of clarity about what I was doing there.

For decades I'd wanted to pay my respects to Thomas Hardy and, in the process, to Robert Russell. Yet I'd never felt strongly enough about it to make the journey until now. It was Russell's death, in large part, that had pushed me to do so. Coming here wasn't prompted by the rereading of Hardy's books, which I'd completed several years before and without feeling the need to reserve a flight to England, but by the loss of a surrogate father who had brought me to those books. That's what inspired me to include these three Dorset days in our trip to England. And I'd come, at the end of an extended vacation, with no expectation other than honoring those two men's places in my life.

But now I found myself compelled—feeling called—to go deeper, to move beyond the boundaries of Thomas Hardy's work in pursuit of truths that might lay buried within it, if I only knew where to look. I felt Russell's presence keenly, urging me to continue my work, to speak my heart and to hear what Hardy's heart might still be trying to say.

"Something I missed." Hardy, I felt, was open to it. And/or I needed to do it. At least that's how I was now understanding his Visitation. There was something here I needed to discover. And I believed he wanted me to touch the relics, follow where they led me. I sat back down.

Beverly, Jason, and I were alone in the house. Jason, sanitizing his hands after touching Bella, was explaining to Beverly the sequence of events that had led Hardy to build an addition to Max Gate, creating space both for his final study and for Emma's attic rooms. The success of his books. The unhappiness with how small his existing study was. The way he felt exposed when anyone came to visit. I knew the story well enough to let the words flow over me. A cloud skimmed past, darkening for just a few seconds the space where I sat, and as bright light returned I remembered the recurring lines from one of Hardy's eeriest poems: "Who's in the next room?—who?"

Who was in the next room, I thought, was the person nowhere to be found in this room. The person Hardy tried so hard to eradicate as a presence in his life when he built this space in which to give himself fully to his work. Even in the reconstruction, Emma was nowhere—not even in a photo—and therefore she seemed to be everywhere. Beside, above, beyond.

Images flooded in the dazzling light. Emma when Hardy first met her, composed and looking away in an oval photo that echoed the shape of her face. Emma a year later in a locket miniature, not quite able to smile. Emma two decades later photographed through a pin-hole camera at Weymouth Pier, dressed in black. Emma old, looking down at an open book, the photo mostly hat. This rush of images slowed like a wheel of fortune and stopped at the same frank, brave face I'd remembered earlier, while standing in the Max Gate driveway. Emma with all her defenses down. Emma plain. Emma.

≋

They met in March 1870. Hardy had expected someone else to receive him at the rectory door. He'd taken four different trains since leaving Bockhampton by morning starlight, then ridden sixteen jouncing miles in a horse-drawn cart, reaching the tiny village of St. Juliot just before seven o'clock with Jupiter visible in the sky. He'd never been to Cornwall. He was cold in the wild coastal wind, had been cold for hours. He'd had little to eat, and spent those hours scribbling notes and drafting a poem on paper he stuffed into his pocket.

The dilapidated church with its cracked tower loomed on the hilltop beside the rectory. Its shadow fell across the pathway leading to the front door. Hardy rang the bell, then rubbed his hands together and blew on them for warmth. Ushered inside, he found neither the rector, whose church Hardy had come all that way to restore, nor the rector's wife waiting for him. Instead, the wife's younger sister, Emma Gifford, was there, dressed in deep dark brown, adorned with masses of corn-colored curls, pale, blue-eyed, and looking uncomfortable in her role as welcomer to a home that wasn't hers. But her appearance spoke to him of grace and gentility, and Emma's gaze was animated, lively with interest as it took in Hardy's yellowish beard, his shabby greatcoat, the bit of blue paper sticking out of his pocket.

She told him her brother-in-law, the reverend Caddell Holder, had been laid up with gout, and her sister Helen was upstairs with him. They would go to meet the Holders as soon as Hardy was ready, then would dine. The table was laid. Emma could see that Hardy was exhausted by his tedious and complicated day's travel. It had been, she thought, "a sort of cross-jump journey like a chess-knight's move." Strangers seldom came to the small, remote village, and she'd been wondering what this architect fellow would be like. She was glad he was there at last, eager—as were most people in the village—for him to arrive so work could finally begin on restoring their long-neglected church.

Emma had expected someone else, too. Or someone different. Despite any local admiration, she'd vowed to keep herself free until the one intended for her arrived. As soon as she saw Hardy, though, she felt sure that she knew him. He was familiar, like someone she'd seen in a dream, and his soft voice with its slight West Country accent charmed her. At first, she took him to be much older than he was. Maybe it was the darkness, or his businesslike appearance, because later, in daylight, he seemed younger. They were, in fact, nearly the same age, both on the verge of thirty and born within five months of each other.

Emma was the daughter of a long-retired solicitor with a gentleman's airs, a serious drinking problem, and few resources. He'd rented accommodations near the Bodmin moors and sent his daughters out to be governesses or ladies' companions. When Helen married Reverend Holder, thirty-five years her senior, she'd brought Emma along. The sisters didn't like each other much, but Emma helped with parish and household duties as the Holders tried hard to find her a husband.

In the days that followed, Emma accompanied Hardy in his preparations for work on the church. She sketched and observed as he made drawings, took measurements, and examined the five church bells inverted and lined up on the transept floor, the carved bench-ends rotting, the ivy-draped old timbers dense with bats and birds, assessing what could be salvaged from the building. She went along on his visits to slate quarries at Tintagel and Penpethy to examine alternative roofing material. Hardy extended his stay. They spent time alone exploring the coast, the fishing port at Boscastle, "the opal and the sapphire of that wandering western sea at Beeny Cliff." Emma, who walked with a limp because of a childhood hip dislocation, was a deft horsewoman, riding Fanny over the landscape as Hardy walked beside her. The bottom of her long riding skirt was flung over her left arm, felt hat turned up at the sides, and she was at ease on her horse, showing the young architect choughs and puffins soaring through ocean spray, the gorged and drenched black cliffs, seeping sunsets, the coast's power to stir heart and soul. They picnicked, and Hardy sketched Emma on her knees—hair loose, curves carefully delineated—reaching into a river for a glass tumbler she'd lost as she rinsed it. There was evening music in the garden and the rectory, where Emma played piano and sang. They read together and spoke of books. She wrote that "scarcely any author and his wife could have had a much more romantic meeting." And Hardy wrote of these days with anguish ("much of my life claims the spot as its key") and adoration ("woman much missed, how you call to me, call to me") after Emma's death forty-two years later, the details etched in memory. "Was there ever a time of such quality, since or before?"

For the next four years, Hardy returned two or three times a year to what he called this Region of Dream and Mystery. They returned to Tintagel, the village and castle so closely linked to the legend of King Arthur and his Knights of the Round Table, and drove a cart to Trebarwith Strand to watch donkeys getting seaweed for local farmers. There were dawdling excursions to the rock-bound cove at Strangles beach, and to visit a neighboring clergyman.

As the work progressed, so did their relationship with each other and with the landscape beyond her home at St. Juliot, pronounced St. Jilt by locals. They corresponded between visits. Emma said she found Hardy a perfectly new subject of study and delight, was charmed with the quickness of his speech and mind. Both wrote of their deepening interest. Emma began to copy out Hardy's manuscripts for him as the early novels took shape. She encouraged and seemed to understand his work, his desire to become a writer and quit architecture.

There's a story that Emma had many suitors among the men of North Cornwall. There's also a story that her family made up the story about all the suitors in North Cornwall so Hardy would feel pressured to propose to Emma. And there's a story that when he proposed, Emma's parents rejected him. This last story seems certainly true, as Hardy never spoke to them again. Resolute, he worked hard at his trades, both architecture and writing, until he could afford marriage.

Whether they were lovers or not over the four years until their marriage, I feel certain—as I do about little else when it comes to Hardy and love—that he was in love with Emma in their early courtship years.

Or, more accurately, that he understood what he felt as being in love. He wrote: "I came back from these first times together with magic in my eyes!"

⁂

Beverly sat at the table in Emma's attic, her hand resting on an antique sewing machine. A slip of daylight through the dormer window warmed her face and saturated her creamy handwoven scarf. The table also held a wicker basket of fabric and a stray, feathery strip of cloth. Folded over a wooden rack, a white quilt seemed to glow at the edge of the light. But beyond it, and throughout the rest of the room, a gloomy duskiness prevailed.

There was a framed etching on the floor, leaning against the wall near the fireplace. Beside a single candlestick on the mantle, a hasty watercolor sketch awaited hanging. The bare wooden floor was stained where a rug had once lain. The effort at refurnishing seemed thwarted, as if Emma's spirit remained in place and forbid the room to resemble anything other than a cell, with nothing in it truly hers, a space to endure rather than thrive.

But Emma had willingly—eagerly—moved herself up there in 1899, writing to a friend, "I sleep in an Attic! My boudoir is my sweet refuge and solace—not a sound scarcely penetrates hither. I see the sun, & stars & moon rise & the birds come to my bird table when a hurricane has not sent them flying."

It was a place of retreat for Emma. Hardy worked below her in the study, and she felt free of him at last. She could read and paint, sew, could talk to her cats if she wanted to without Hardy's sour disapproval. Being up there only made explicit what had been implicit in recent years: trapped together at Max Gate, they barely spoke, barely had anything like an intimate life together. They could go out, travel together, attend plays—they could do the husband-and-wife thing in public— but they couldn't be at home with each other.

How had the Hardys come from the romance and the magic of their early days to this in their twenty-five years of married life? His reserve had become complete withdrawal, his restraint impassivity. Her vitality had become rage, her expressiveness self-torment. By the time she moved to the attic, Emma was referring to Hardy in her writings as The W.M., for The Wicked Man. We know this because a manuscript Emma had written, *Some Recollections*, was found after her death. Hardy had included eighteen of its pages in his self-ghostwritten biography, where I encountered her descriptions of their courtship. That was material of which Hardy clearly approved. But he'd also failed to print fifty-six other pages, which surfaced in 1961, revealing the depths of Emma's loathing: "I can scarcely think that love proper, and enduring, is in the nature of men."

Standing there in the attic, I understood that it was impossible not to ask if their love was ever real romance and magic rather than literary romance and magic. Whether it was all about their fantasies and imaginings, with little actuality to their connection. Things dreamt, of comelier hue than things beholden!

While I believe this couple at thirty was primed to fall in love, was swept away by the fairy-tale elements of the setting, I also believe in Hardy's line, his sense that love when it struck like that was a kind of joyous spell, a benevolent sorcery. I believe in his ardor, as well as his compulsion to write of it. Both real.

But I can't help wondering if the charm began to weaken well before they came near the separation enacted here. Well before the construction of Max Gate, never a home built to please or accommodate Emma, who didn't want to live in Dorset, let alone in a house like this. I was thinking particularly of the four years after their initial meetings and before their marriage. When Hardy was perhaps being manipulated—and requiring manipulation—to propose. Could it be that there were factors other than finances inhibiting him? I remembered what Sharon Taylor had intimated about Tryphena.

"It's good that Emma had a place of her own," Beverly said. "But it seems like a very interior space. Compare it to his, looking out into the garden. He's awash in light, he's free to move all over the house, and she's up here, battling the dark and straining for a glimpse of a bird."

Seeing Beverly there, her face now half in light and half in darkness, I remembered her moving through a yoga routine in the yurt on an early spring afternoon. This must have been six years ago, shortly after we'd made the decision to move back to the city. She stood on one leg like a heron, then segued into a deep bend and settled down to the floor. As I'd watched, light from the arc of windows in front of her and from the skylight above her seemed also to be emanating from within her, all meeting at a point just above her head. She was a being who charged herself with light, and who in turn charged the world around her with it. We would move to a place by the river and filled with light from the south and the east, but it would be a different kind of light altogether. What I'd seen in our yurt was seared into memory. I would carry within me the sight of my wife as the nexus of inner and outer light, her skin glowing.

Beverly ran her fingers across the base of the sewing machine. "She needed to get away, but she got the scruff. Doing the work she liked, her sewing and painting and writing, needs light. It's so sad."

Jason, who'd stayed on the first floor to check his e-mail and take care of some Max Gate paperwork, was now coming up to rejoin us. "Questions?" he said from the stairwell. When he saw us, he stopped. "Interrupting, I see. Sorry."

"I was just thinking about how hard it must have been for Emma to climb up here," I said. "I mean, at her age and with her lame leg."

"And I was thinking about how hard it must have been for Emma to endure the winters up here." Beverly pointed to the fireplace. "Even with some heat."

Jason nodded, and let the quiet settle, still not sure if he should retreat. Instead, compromising, he looked down and said, "I don't come to the attic much. You know, Emma used to fire off letters to the editors of various newspapers. Wrote them here. Full of optimism, they were. Spirit. Not what you'd expect. In one she wrote that 'in one or two generations nearly every person would in some way or other be a maker of happiness.' Try to think about that whenever I'm in this room."

"What do you think she meant by that?" I asked.

"She'd become deeply religious by then. Very Christian. Faith in the future. Goodness of people. As Hardy drifted further from religion and from her."

"So she was expressing hope," Beverly said. "Despite everything. It's remarkable."

"It is. And quite moving. Hardy was hardly a maker of happiness." Jason hesitated, then added, "Not in his personal life and not in his books. Emma began to think of him as evil."

"The Wicked Man," I said. "But it wasn't wickedness in him, or evil. Maybe Hardy couldn't be a maker of happiness because he couldn't bring himself to risk it. Closed himself off, hid himself away, didn't believe in it anymore."

"Perhaps that's so."

"Do I remember right—that this is where she died?"

"Quite suddenly. Early morning in November." Jason pointed to the other attic room. "Dolly Gale was in there, came through here as usual around eight o'clock. Found Emma moaning. Terribly ill. Ran down to interrupt Hardy in his study. Dolly told people that he ordered her to straighten her collar before he left the room. Climbed the stairs, found Emma unconscious. She died as he was saying 'Em, Em, don't you know me?'" Jason looked at us with real sorrow in his eyes. "I always wondered if that was the first time Hardy had been in this room since she'd moved up."

The bare bones recital of Emma's death made it all the more haunting. Beverly and I took one last look around the room and headed down behind Jason.

11

Beverly said she'd meet me in Hardy's Nut Walk after taking a restroom break. I went outside and paused on the small porch, aware of traffic sounds from the A35 nearby but thinking about the Hardys' final moments together. The shock, Hardy's futile attempt to keep his distance by sustaining formality and order (straighten your collar!), and his outcry focused not quite on Emma but on whether she recognized him. *Em, Em, don't you know me?*

This sad, sudden scene—"Never to bid good-bye," Hardy had written in the first of his mourning poems for Emma—confirmed for me one answer to the question of what Hardy had missed. He longed to be known, and feared he never was. He'd felt it from the very first, cast aside as dead, the life inside him invisible to those in charge of it. He was driven to hide himself, yet terrified of not being recognized. Frantic for love, he couldn't do the one thing most necessary to love: reveal himself, give himself. Or as Beverly had said before we went for our walk yesterday, could he be lost now because he could never lose himself when alive? Though he always felt compelled to hide, what terrified him as the Hardys' life together ended was that the person with whom he'd spent forty-two years didn't—couldn't—know him. Who, then, could? It tormented his spirit still.

I walked past the conservatory and Middle Lawn toward the hedge-covered brick wall at the perimeter of the property. At the lawn's edge, there was a hexagonal table, bare except for a ceramic shoe meant to contain flowers. I imagined Jason drank his morning tea there while sitting on the single folding chair and working on the problem of love's geometry in Hardy's novels, thinking about Miss Petherwin choosing among her three suitors in *The Hand of Ethelberta*.

In an alcove within the overgrowth Hardy had placed his Druid stone. It "broods in the garden white and lone," and marks the start of the Nut Walk. He loved strolling here morning and evening between the rows of beech trees he'd planted. "I set every tree in my June time, and now they obscure the sky." Hardy felt so attached to his trees that, like young Jude Fawley, he couldn't trim them, thereby imagining he was sparing them pain.

Entering the Nut Walk changed the entire feel of being at Max Gate. It was darker inside, cooler, thick with the smells of nature left to its own ways. I remembered such dank presence of growth and death from our years in the woods, especially in early June when the unseen life hidden around us seemed even more riotous than the life thriving before our eyes.

Traffic hushed and I could hear the rich phrases of a song thrush's music, the lush throaty song of a blackbird. The thick foliage was sprinkled with wood anemone. A narrow footworn path led through shadows toward bursts of sunlight farther down. Alone here, it was easy to believe that Hardy—as he'd written after Emma's death—thought he'd seen her standing at the end of this "alley of bending boughs." It felt like a place where specters would thrive. Looking as deeply into it as I could, I saw the perspective shrink toward a point of darkness like the mouth of a cave.

And there was Thomas Hardy.

All I could do at first was stare. His form wavered a bit, as though backlit by fire. Then I realized it was because my eyes were watering—whether from not blinking, from the odd breeze at the mouth of the

Nut Walk, or from emotion, I couldn't say for sure. I shut and rubbed my eyes. When I opened them again Hardy hadn't vanished. So this was, I understood, another Visitation.

I felt dizzy and took a few steps backward to regain balance. I'd never had a cluster of Visitations before or repeated Visits by the same figure. I felt confused, for the first time in my world of Visitations, about who was Visiting whom. Was Hardy the Visitor or was I?

He was now bent at the waist and seemed to be digging, or turning over loose soil. I wasn't sure if I should approach him. After watching for a moment, I noticed that the more he worked, the barer the area around him became. Trees were disappearing. Light began flowing in around him. That's when I realized Hardy was taking us backward in time. The trees were ungrowing. And, if I was correct, we'd soon be at the point where he'd begun planting them in 1885. I saw the windswept ridge where Hardy stood surveying his land, the thousands of small Austrian pines and beeches he'd bought to plant, the house slowly taking shape, then his figure in an upstairs window looking north over the valley and seeing Stinsford Church, where all of this would eventually lead, his deepest wishes about Home made manifest.

I'd been holding my breath. As I exhaled, Hardy straightened up, put his boot on the shovel blade's foot rest, and seemed to stare at me. The wind picked up. "Wish it," I thought he said. Wish it? Missed? Then, spoken more slowly, I thought I heard "as you wish it." The light in the Nut Walk changed again, began darkening, and Hardy's rustling whispery voice filled the space between us. This time, what it said was clear. "Nothing is as you wish it."

As he had done in his parents' bedroom yesterday, Hardy held my gaze. His features coalesced as though to provide me with certainty about what I saw, and thus about what I'd heard. I could even make out the waxed, delicately curled tips of his gray moustache. Hardy in his early sixties, around the time Emma died. I lifted my hand but he was already gone.

≋

I stayed where I was. Maybe Hardy planned to return yet again. But then maybe he'd show up next by the Pet Cemetery or before the carriage house, in the garden, under the sundial on the east turret. As that thought occurred, the world outside the Nut Walk reasserted itself. I heard a car horn, a trash truck, voices in the neighborhood. Then I recognized the whistling call of a meadowlark, which was how Beverly always let me know she was looking for me, and a moment later saw her appear at the entrance to the Nut Walk.

When I started telling her what had happened, she stopped me and suggested that we walk through the Nut Walk together as I spoke. We took a few steps and I pointed out where I'd been standing when Hardy appeared. Then I began to cry. Beverly embraced me, and that made my crying intensify.

I mentioned earlier that I'm still learning to accommodate the on-going, persistent results of the lesions that have damaged my neurological functioning. As my cognitive powers had been altered (all right: dimin-ished), my emotional responses had become less repressed. Over time, it has seemed like an even trade, the 20 percent drop in IQ compensated for by a 20 percent rise in emotional disinhibition. So I cry. A lot. And suddenly. Like young Tom Hardy weeping at traditional folk song lyrics, I cry when I hear classic Broadway show tunes. Sometimes all it takes is the first two or three notes of the melody, even before the lyrics begin. I also cry at old standards like "They Can't Take That Away From Me" or "Fever," at doo-wop and early rock 'n' roll (I've even cried hearing Bobby Darin's 1958 hit "Splish Splash"). The soaring notes of a cello solo or the falling notes of a string quartet. Harry Belafonte makes me cry! And it's not just about music. I can cry when Ichiro Suzuki makes a gorgeous catch and throw from right field or when a great blue heron lands on the top of a cottonwood tree. Or, combining music and move-ment, when Apolo Anton Ohno does the samba with Julianne Hough to "I Like to Move It" on *Dancing with the Stars*. When I entered the newly remodeled attic office in my daughter's Chicago home and saw its array of purple walls, its abundance of family photos, the sun pouring through its skylights—its essential Beckaness—I burst into tears. Later that day, I also cried while telling her the story of how my uncle had helped with my college expenses when scholarships and work-study payments weren't adequate, and while listening to the "Cooking with Papa" playlist of songs she'd assembled for our times together in the kitchen. She's used to it by now, and so is Beverly. I can get all teary sometimes just seeing my wife's smile, or hearing her sweet alto voice join in on a song I didn't even realize I was singing out loud. And by her sweet embrace. This is not the way I used to be. But this is who I am and it's pointless to resist or deny it.

As she held me, and the emotional storm that had welled up began to subside, I remembered going to Robert Russell's office one spring afternoon in 1969 and announcing, "Love is a maelstrom of fire!" I'd felt certain I'd found the key to understanding Thomas Hardy and his novels. All his stormy, fiery, explosive characters—unpredictable, fervid, ultimately destructive in the grip of love and desire. Love made life possible, sure, but it also had the power to obliterate, and that part was Hardy's fixation. Couldn't stop writing about it. The phrase "a maelstrom of fire" came from a scene early in *Two on a Tower*, his ninth novel. Lovers studying "a cyclone in the sun" through a telescope see the blazing globe as "a maelstrom of fire." There it was! I'd read enough Hardy by then to realize that this was the perfect metaphor for love as he understood it. A maelstrom of fire, hypnotizing, life-giving, but self-immolating, a mortal danger. Russell rocked back in his chair as I spoke, leaned forward to feel around his desk and locate his pipe, went through his customary lighting ceremony, and said, "Leave it to Hardy to give it to us twice: a cyclone in the sun *and* a maelstrom of fire."

In Beverly's arms, the phrase "love is a maelstrom of fire" came together for me with "Nothing is as you wish it" and "Something I missed," and I felt Hardy's despair settle like a deepening shadow around us in the Nut Walk. It had not been Hardy's appearance that triggered my crying. It had been Beverly's return, her willingness to share my experience, the reality of her touch after Hardy's Visitation. Because of her, I didn't miss love. Because of her, what I wished for has happened. And I knew how fortunate I was.

We began walking through the space that had separated me from Hardy during his Visitation. It's not that I expected to find scorched earth or overturned soil or Hardy's bootprints, but I wanted to study the ground, embed it in memory. He had imagined and created this Nut Walk as he imagined and created *The Mayor of Casterbridge* or *The Woodlanders*, while living here. In a way it felt like I was reading him afresh by walking here with Beverly in the light of all we'd learned so far.

⊜

We had one final stop to make before saying good-bye to Jason and leaving Max Gate: the Pet Cemetery. Beginning in 1890 when their beloved black retriever Moss died, the Hardys buried their dogs and cats, some with headstones engraved by Hardy himself, in a shady spot on the western side of the garden. There are tombstones for the dogs Moss and Wessex, after whose death Hardy could no longer bear to have dogs. The cats Chips and Comfy are memorialized there along with Hardy's favorite cat, Kitesey, and Emma's adored albino cat, Snowdove. A few smaller stones are scattered around the plot, under trees and beside stumps. Beverly took photos from various angles, moving carefully, respectful of what this place meant.

The Hardys' devotion to these animals has been seen as comical, macabre, pathetic. It's been seen as a substitute for love they couldn't give to each other, or to a child. They had a cat named Kiddleywinkempoops! Their dog had a terrible temper! There were saucers of milk everywhere! Their pampered cat ate Hardy's heart!

But I get it. I was raised without pets of any kind by a mother terrified of dirt or germs and a butcher father who slaughtered poultry for a living. My daughter, dedicated all her life to protecting and rescuing animals, taught me to see them as she did, open myself to them, begin to understand. But it wasn't until I got together with Beverly and moved to the woods that I lost my heart altogether, in the way that Hardy seems to have lost his, to the animals who shared our life. Particularly cats. When we married, Beverly had two shelter cats, Zak and Zola, and soon we took in my daughter's cat, Zeppo, so he could have twenty acres over which to rule. By the time Zak died at eighteen I loved him so powerfully that I dug his grave myself, dislodging boulders and using a pick and spade to gouge out the diced basalt and stone. It took hours. I was drenched in sweat and having balance problems when I bent over to dig and when I knelt to scoop with my hands, which became crusted with the dark soil where Zak would rest. But I needed to do this, and do it myself. When Zeppo died and we continued to hear his voice haunting the landscape, Beverly sought to contain her grief by writing her first haiku:

> Small cry at corner
> in rising spring vapor
> ghost cat of my heart.

So the Pet Cemetery didn't seem strange, just touching. It revealed an emotional expressiveness I'd been looking for in Hardy's life, to match what I'd found in some of his most compelling characters and inspired poems. With the Nut Walk on the eastern edge of the property and the Pet Cemetery on the western edge, there seemed to be a borderland of phantom life, edges where—unlike the interior of Max Gate—a residue of the real and best-concealed Hardy survived. Where love and passion lived. Not long after Emma died, Hardy had written to a friend that his saddest times were at dusk when he crossed the garden and came to the place where the Nut Walk begins, and where he recalled her walking with the cat trotting faithfully behind her. And not long after Snowdove died, Hardy wrote about him in a way that anticipated the poems he'd write after Emma's death, with genuine sorrow and regret, haunted by the small grave "showing in the autumn shade that you moulder where you played."

We returned to the house. Jason wasn't in any of the ground-floor rooms, and we didn't want to call out in case he'd begun working in his first-floor study. So we signed the guest book, left a note of thanks, and got as far as the porch before we heard him bounding down the stairs.

"That was quick," he said. "Saw you go into the Pet Cemetery, thought I had time to find this and copy down all the details." He waved a sheet of paper, then turned around and stood by the desk. "Remembered something you might be interested in. Wait just half a moment. Almost done."

"We're not in a rush," Beverly said.

"Yes. Well." When he finished writing, he faced us again and smiled. "Backstory: After you left the attic, I thought about this show that's on tonight. Adaptation of *Far from the Madding Crowd*. Just a few scenes, really. Outdoors, raise funds for the Hardy Theatre Company. Well and good. Over by Lulworth Cove, which figures in the action."

"You're kidding," I said.

Jason looked puzzled. "Why would I do that?"

I shook my head and apologized. "It's just that we stumbled onto a rehearsal for it yesterday afternoon. Our B&B is nearby."

"Oh? Anthony and Nan Swain's place?" When we nodded, Jason said, "Wouldn't be surprised if they're at the show tonight too." He handed over his note with details of the performance.

"Thank you," I said. "I'm glad you remembered this."

"Triggered by telling you about the morning Emma died. Remembered Hardy had left her the evening before so he could go into Dorchester to watch a rehearsal. A play made from one of his books. *The Trumpet-Major*, I think. But that led me to think of tonight's play, you see? If you're still in Dorchester."

"We're here till midday tomorrow. Then on to London for the night, and home."

"So. Maybe see you tonight, then."

"Wouldn't miss it," Beverly said, to my great relief.

12

Our plan had been to stop next at Hardy's grave in Stinsford Churchyard a mile and a half away. But now that felt wrong. As we left Max Gate and stood by the brick wall to take a last set of photos, I said, "This was like visiting a monument to the failure of love."

Beverly turned on the camera. "I know what you mean."

"And now we go to where his heart is buried? It all seems so grim and mournful."

"Well, is there any place you think love actually flourished for him? Where he was lighthearted and joyful?"

Of course! We needed to backtrack to the one place where love may have succeeded for Thomas Hardy. Succeeded, at least, for a while, dark though that place might sometimes be. The heath and forest by his Bockhampton cottage. The ponds and fields, the hills. We needed to go where his deepest wishes formed, and ultimately where he began to understand what he'd missed. I needed to feel the presence of Hardy in love. Well, something like that.

Even if only some of the story we'd heard about Hardy and Tryphena was correct, then the landscape between his cottage and Puddletown was its setting. The romance of a couple "Lit by a living love / The wilted world knew nothing of" would have happened sometime after

Hardy returned from his five-year interlude in London at the age of twenty-seven, but before he married Emma at thirty-four: 1867 to 1874.

When we'd been at the cottage yesterday, I was focused—when I could focus at all—mostly on Hardy's childhood, and on his writing life. But he was there when love struck, too. Cassie Pole, Tryphena Sparks, perhaps others as well. He also lived there, with occasional trips to Cornwall, for the four years it took him and Emma finally to marry after their initial meeting.

Hardy may have been effective at containing the evidence, but we still needed to return. It would be as Hardy put it in his poem "A Spot," in which he imagined people like us coming there to be in the presence of his great love:

> Lonely shepherd souls
> Who bask amid these knolls
> May catch a faery sound
> On sleepy noontides from the ground:
> "O not again
> Till Earth outwears
> Shall love like theirs
> Suffuse this glen!"

Beverly gave the camera to me, and stood by the unruly hedge that overhung Hardy's brick wall. She was dappled in shadow and wearing her charcoal-gray, thigh-length, lined parka and the creamy scarf she wove herself. And I will never forget—to paraphrase a Hardy poem—the full-souled sweetness warming her smile. She was with me on this mission, on what some might consider a wild goose chase, and ready for whatever came next.

⁂

Tryphena Sparks was sixteen and knew what she wanted to do. Bright, vibrant, a little sassy, she'd talked since she was eleven about becoming a teacher and eventually a headmistress.

Already she was working as a pupil-teacher in the girls' section of Puddletown elementary school. She could be playful and charming, but she wasn't coy, and there was little of the child left in her, especially now that her mother was dying and she was helping her sister Rebecca care for her. Through the long hours at home by the bedside, Tryphena suppressed her natural exuberance. Once outside again, she was animated and eager.

Tryphena had dark eyes with laughter in them, had thick, bold eyebrows, ears without lobes, full lips, heaps of lustrous black hair. She was built close to the ground and moved with a straightforward nimbleness. Her voice was rich with feeling, deeper and more musical than either of her sisters'. Good friends and family called her Triffie or Phena.

When her cousin Tom moved back from London in 1867, he seemed desolate. Her heart went out to him, a warmth and compassion he badly needed. They recognized something familiar in each other.

Tryphena knew—because he'd told her over and over—that Hardy had felt sickened by London's summer heat and stench from the Thames running directly beneath his window. But even before that, when the work of preparing a site for a railroad cutting required him to oversee the removal of coffins and bones from St. Pancras cemetery, he'd begun to feel weakened and depressed. For a year or more he was getting worn out by tedious drawing and recopying assignments, dull architecture work mixed with long afterhours of reading and study, theater going, making the rounds of museums and galleries, educating himself. He'd been writing poems for several years, poems no one wanted to publish, and had begun work on a novel. A romance with a neighboring servant girl fizzled. Cooped up in the office, in his apartment, in the city, he was fading for lack of light and lack of nature. He didn't do well on his own. When John Hicks, the Dorchester architect he'd been apprenticed to as a youth, needed an assistant, Hardy seized the chance to return.

Like all of Hardy's friends, Tryphena was shocked by his pallor. His hair was lank, thinning. He seemed to have shrunk two inches. It was clear he needed to be home.

Throughout the summer, Hardy walked to Hicks's office in Dorchester and back. He also walked across the heath and scrubland to Puddletown for visits. It was just two miles, bypassing an unplowed sheep pasture, the Coomb eweleaze. Sometimes he encountered a few wild heath-ponies, and the sight of them—equal parts waking dream and living memory—filled him with joy. He loved being surrounded by the sound of rustling heather. Birds flushed at his approach. Marsh harriers circled above him. He could feel himself returning to life, feel life returning to him.

Hardy was comfortable, secure again in the Puddletown house with the river sparkling in front, where in the past he used to visit Tryphena's older sisters, her brothers, his aunt and uncle. It had—except for that brief banishment after the incident with his cousin Rebecca—been like a second home for him, cheerful and warm, spirited, musical, and in London he'd missed it almost as much as the cottage at Bockhampton.

Now his visits became more frequent, full of conversation rather than youthful games. And, after paying his respects to his aunt, totally focused on Tryphena. When the nearby church's chimes rang, he would cock his head and listen closely, hand raised to stop any further chitchat, the church architect at work. Soon Hardy noticed that he didn't have to signal his desire for quiet. Tryphena knew, just from being close to him, what her cousin wanted.

Tryphena was happy to talk about whatever Hardy was interested in. Or to learn French from him, since it might be useful in her teaching career. He had plans, too. Once, she remembered, he'd thought he might become a clergyman. But he'd given that up, discouraged about being able to attend the university and, apparently, losing his belief in God. Now he was devoted to writing, would earn his living as a novelist and at the same time secretly fulfill his calling as a poet. He'd grown up with stories all around him, and characters no one in London knew about, a rustic world that was beginning to vanish. As he spoke of these things, he gazed at Tryphena as though memorizing her every feature, line, gesture. Or as though not actually seeing her.

She liked the long walks they began to take, was grateful to get away from home and her mother's final suffering. It rained often that summer, but the weather didn't deter them. In the woods and on the heath, Hardy's thoughts raced. His ideas for the novel caromed between memories of his experience in London and scenes of country life. He sprang ahead of Tryphena and turned to face her, walking backward as he told her about the main character, humble Will Strong, and his failed attempts to court a landowner's daughter. Hardy reached out for Tryphena's hand in his excitement about Will Strong going to London and training as an architect, enduring loneliness there, cast upon the uncaring city with nothing but his brains and his courage and his feeling of dedication so he could return worthy of Miss Allancourt's hand. Hardy pulled Tryphena down beside him on a fallen oak and proclaimed himself in favor of radical politics. There were outbursts against the hypocrisy of the upper class, tirades about the denial of education to the working class and to women. Sitting by Rushy Pond or Green Hill Pond, resting under trees in the eweleaze, he talked about books he'd read in London and was reading now, or reminisced about hearing Charles Dickens read onstage, or recited a list of phrases and strange words he'd come across and written down in his journal, or called himself a Socialist, talking about strikes and demonstrations. Then he quieted down and said of course he wasn't really a Socialist. But, he said, shouting to frighten a flock of blackbirds, his novel would be a Socialist Novel! A love story, too. And there would be folk in it that Tryphena would recognize. Shakespeare showed how important it was to have folk in the thing.

Tryphena understood what was happening before Hardy did. And it was she who initiated their first kiss. They were in the eweleaze, which had become one of their favorite places to walk or to sit under the trees and talk while the sheep grazed and the thriving lambs played. It was a lush, rolling upland field, isolated and quiet except for the occasional bleating of the sheep or shift in the wind. That day, Tryphena had not let go of Hardy's hand when he pulled her down to listen to his latest disquisition about abused servants in London homes. It had taken him a few minutes to notice. Soon she had "kindled love's fitful ecstasies!" and Hardy was "transport-tossed."

By summer's end, writing, being at home where he could eat his mother's cooking and hear again the song of the nightingales, spending time with Tryphena ("Two fields, a wood, a tree, / Nothing now more malign / Lies between you and me"), walking to and from his old architecture office in Dorchester, working on church restorations, he felt himself restored as well.

⁂

Beverly and I detoured into Dorchester to assemble a picnic lunch. Since the food co-op was near the Dorset County Museum, we went there too and bought a selection of Hardy's poetry to take into the heath and forest. Then we drove to Higher Bockhampton and the Thorncombe Wood parking lot near Hardy's cottage. Our first destination this time, I thought, should be Rushy Pond, about a ten-minute walk.

At the lot's far end we took a path that climbed steeply into the trees. I had the lunch and water bottles, our vests and hats, a picnic blanket Nan had lent us, maps, notebook, guidebook and Hardy's poetry all stuffed into a backpack, and was sweaty by the time the trail leveled out. I stopped to adjust the straps and shrug the pack in place.

The landscape was no longer Hardy's untameable wild. But it was thriving and full of life in the late spring weather. The trail opened into a groomed glade of tall beech. Beverly identified the songs of robins and wrens, a group of warblers, chaffinch. We saw two other couples ahead of us, and a family with three kids, but they all took the path that led toward Hardy's cottage. We followed the one toward Rushy Pond.

Soon we came to the remnants of an old metal boundary fence. A little farther along there was a sturdy wooden gate, recently attached, and a notice board with a fading flyer announcing the Five-Year Thomas Hardy Egdon Heath Restoration Project. The famous setting of so many classic novels would be returned to its original, timeless state to be enjoyed by all! But it looked like the project had stalled after a few trees and rhododendron were cut. A gray squirrel darted under the fence.

We stayed on the path as it led uphill. Packs of young silver birch were trying to become woodland, but mostly what we saw was bracken. When we reached Rushy Pond, at the highest part of the heath, it was both smaller and less sheltered than I'd anticipated. But it was also beautiful, open as though eager to fill itself with sky, cloud, sun, moon. The water's surface that morning mirrored a few bordering trees and overhanging limbs, the smooth drift of clouds. It was a place of reflection, all right, as well as a watering hole for whatever came by. Dragonflies and damselflies, maybe other species if we were quiet enough.

We sat on one of the small log benches near the pond's edge and began unpacking our lunch. Apples, a chunk of hard Woolsery goat cheese, a small bag of greens, gluten-free herb and onion crackers, a mix of nuts, a couple of chocolate cookies. After we spread the meal out on the blanket, I figured the time had come to read "At Rushy-Pond" aloud.

A terse, wintry poem, it opens with the image of a half moon reflected on the pond's "frigid face." A cold north wind sets the moon's reflection in motion, first stretching it to an oval shape, then corkscrewing it before allowing it to settle again. Hardy, sitting where we're sitting now, doesn't care to look up at the real moon because the dreamy image he's seen in the pond recalls the memory of a scene that once took place here. The poem's heart is in this recollection, and Hardy can't look away. "Once, in a secret year, / I had called a woman to me / from across this water, ardently." She came to him and he "practiced to keep her near." But their relationship broke off, "the last weak love-words had been said / And ended was her time." Their love blanched from fiery red to white, became a "wraith," a phantom of its feverish urgency. The remnants of it and of her beauty were, he thinks, like "the troubled orb in the pond's sad shine": faded, distorted, caught as in a funhouse mirror.

It's a sorrowful poem about love's failure to endure, and it closes with an emphatic, hard matter-of-factness: "Her days dropped out of mine." But that hardness feels forced, a willed display of macho bravado. It was fun while it lasted; a guy's gotta move on. I don't believe it, and neither does the poem because, after all, the memory endures so strongly. Her days didn't drop out of his, only her presence did. She, at her most beloved, is still with him. Fiercely embedded in his memory.

The poem's—and the poet's—heart and soul, the full force of its feeling, is in the poem's dead center, its vision of love in bloom, of secrets and trysts when he called to her ardently and she came to him from across this water. Hardy badly wanted firm closure on his feelings, and on his poem too, so he obeyed the demands of form, the lure of a thudding, tight end. But, as with so much that of Hardy, the evidence left for readers to find within the work convinces us to doubt what's being said. This was the love of his life, and he let it go. It was a pattern throughout his long life, falling for and tiring of women, his passion always self-consuming.

When I'd finished reading "At Rushy-Pond," Beverly took the book and reread the poem silently. Then she set it aside and gazed over the water.

"I wonder when he wrote that," she said, watching as a robin hopped near the margin of the woods.

I picked up the book and turned to the notes in back. "Wow. Looks like it was included in the last book he published, when he was eighty-five."

She nodded. "That makes sense to me. He couldn't let it go and it never lost its grip on him either. He's looking back a long way but it feels so immediate, doesn't it? And so full of regret." She reached for the book. "For what, though, that's the question." She studied the poem for a while. "Do you think it could be inhibition he regrets? Its impact is everywhere in the poem, hedging things in, tamping them down. Look: the pond is 'heath-hemmed,' the moon is 'half-grown' and later it's 'weary,' the pond has a 'sad shine,' their love-words are 'weak,' her beautiful plumage is 'blurred.' Everything's stunted or exhausted. Held in, held back. And so is he. It's like he's cooperated in his own neutralizing or something, let himself be stopped, and he knows it."

"Does it seem like he feels guilty?"

"I didn't sense guilt so much as ongoing torment, you know? A loss of spirit from which he didn't recover. It's hard to look back and find yourself wanting. At fault."

"It's enough to keep someone restless for all time."

We sat side-by-side on the bench, watching the pond and eating. Were we, as I felt we were, in one of the essential places in Hardy's love story? The work said so, I supposed. Poems, and so much of the turbulent, feral energy among the lovers in *The Return of the Native* revolving right around this spot.

There was a rustling sound from the margins of the trees in front of us but it stopped before anyone appeared. I hoped our isolation wouldn't be interrupted yet. I felt on the verge of making a vital connection to what Hardy had missed, and why he believed nothing was as he wished it. I took back the book and read the rest of the note about "At Rushy-Pond." It referred me to another poem, "On a Heath," which opened with the sound of a woman's skirt rustling through the heather. How strange that the rustling I'd just heard would overlap with the rustling I'd just read about. I was going to mention this to Beverly when she gasped.

Slowly, like actors wandering onstage, a pair of heath-ponies emerged from the woods. The first was gray, almost white where the sunlight caught his coat and flowing mane. His head had a bit of a crest and his powerful shoulder rippled where he stood. The best adjective to describe the way he looked was the one that combined Robust and Sturdy: Hardy.

His large eyes found us, small ears perked, long tail swishing. The second pony stopped before fully leaving the shelter of the trees. She was chestnut, stocky and broad, a strong filly, with an expression that struck me as calm, even kind.

Without taking her eyes off them, Beverly reached for my hand and squeezed it. The chestnut pony began walking again, coming into the light. They were both about four feet tall, and the gray was waiting for her to catch up. It was clear that they'd seen us and decided we were all right, no threat. They grazed as they approached Rushy Pond.

"Aren't they beautiful?" Beverly whispered.

I expected them to stop at the pond's edge. But they kept walking until they were hock-deep in the water. First the male, then the female lowered their heads and drank.

No doubt these heath-ponies were part of the same Thomas Hardy Egdon Heath Restoration Project that sponsored the gate in the woods and the clearing of invasive species. But there was no way that, on its own, was an adequate explanation for what just happened. Not for me.

As we'd eaten and talked about the poem, as the sense grew stronger that we were in a place where Hardy had known love, I was thinking about his experience during that summer of 1867. He'd come home from London sick, almost ravaged by the combination of things he'd gone through. Then he recovered, or was restored, and we were in the epicenter of where that happened. It must have felt miraculous to Hardy, magical and life-changing. All of this resonated for me with my own experience of beginning to heal when Beverly and I got together, when I moved into the woods with her, when love took hold of me. When I was slowly restored to some rickety semblance of mobility, balance, coherence.

I knew what Hardy had found. All I could do, at that moment, was grieve for what he then lost again. For what he had missed.

The gray pony climbed out of the pond and shook himself free of water. He raised and lowered his head a couple of times. Then he approached us, moving with slow certainty, until he was right before us. Without giving it another thought, I held out one of our apples and he took it from my hand.

13

I'm not sure how long we stayed with the ponies because time disappeared while they were there. They were calm, unhurried, curious. The gray one nudged and nuzzled at my backpack on the ground while the chestnut listened to Beverly's whispered praises. But then, hearing before we did the distant chatter and squeal of children headed toward the pond, both ponies turned away and ambled into the woods.

We packed up and followed a trail northeast toward Puddletown. According to our map, several different routes would get us there, but we wanted to stop at Coomb eweleaze along the way. It was a farmer's unremarkable sheep pasture, and had been that for more than a century, but it might as well have had a round blue plaque nailed to one of its trees saying "This field is reputed to be where the lovers in THOMAS HARDY'S poem IN A EWELEAZE NEAR WEATHERBURY shared love's fitful ecstasies."

It certainly meant more to Hardy than just a place where he and Tryphena would make love. According to poem after poem, Hardy as a child would "lie upon the leaze and watch the sky." Or he'd pass the hills and see "the leaze smiling on and on"; he'd walk the paths across it and savor "summer's green wonderwork." He danced upon it. And then came the months when Tryphena joined him there: "Under boughs of brushwood / Linking tree and tree / In a shade of lushwood, / There caressed we!"

As Beverly and I crossed a series of stiles and followed the paths, I thought that Hardy had chosen the leaze for his trysts because of its youthful associations with wonder and delight, private joys, ease. He thought it all would never end (Thine for ever!), just as he'd wanted childhood never to end.

But love with Tryphena didn't bring him wonder and delight and joy and ease for long. Love never did, with anyone in Hardy's life. He'd fall in love hard, but wake one morning and realize he no longer thought his beloved was so wonderful. He no longer felt bedazzled by what he'd thought were her charms. "The prize I drew is a blank to me!" Others began to look more stirring.

After little more than a year, the fire Tryphena kindled in Hardy had dwindled and the living love that lit the spot where they'd been together was dying. "The vows of man and maid are frail as filmy gossamere." Tryphena was in trouble at Puddletown School, reproved for neglect of duty. She'd been needed more and more at home until her mother died in November 1868, so Tryphena was often absent, distracted. And since she saw as much of Hardy as she could, word got around and the young pupil-teacher's reputation was compromised. By year's end, she'd been replaced by another pupil-teacher and had moved on to a small village school at Coryates, not far from Weymouth.

Hardy missed their routine, missed having her available to listen as he spoke about his novel-in-progress and his plans. But he didn't miss Tryphena herself, had already felt his interest in her and his desire for her weakening. She was lively enough but she wasn't worldly enough. At this time, he wrote a poem ominously punning on Tryphena's surname, Sparks: "From the letters of her name / The radiance has waned away!"

Though he took the occasional temporary assignment from an architect in Weymouth, and so could visit her in her new location, Hardy wasn't sorry that Tryphena couldn't risk being seen with him about town except in the most public of settings. They sat by the shore at a discreet distance from each other, maintaining strict decorum as they talked and as he walked her back to her rooms. They no longer snuck away, even when they were both at home in Bockhampton and Puddletown.

Hardy found that he liked being free again, meeting women in Weymouth for boating excursions or at dances. He began his romance with the pretty maid, Cassie Pole, back near Bockhampton. Sometimes, though, as when he went rowing alone or with friends in Weymouth, he would lament what he'd lost: she of a bygone vow. Hardy seemed to wallow in woefulness, using the loss of love—as he'd used the finding of love—to inspire poetry. It was love, not Tryphena, that he missed.

He and Tryphena didn't officially end things then, but about a year after her mother's death Tryphena was accepted by Stockwell Normal College in south London. Her plans were back on track. She began the two-year teacher training program there in January 1870. Hardy traveled to Cornwall three months later and met Emma.

⚏

At Coomb eweleaze there were utility poles and a new blue barn in the distance, the sound of a large tractor and a barking brindled boxer that didn't appreciate our wandering into the field. But it was still possible to imagine how this spot looked to Hardy when he brought Tryphena to it. Hedged, with heath rising at one end, woods at another, and a flat area where the dances must have taken place, as in *The Return of the Native*. No one in sight or likely to appear without warning, only the occasional cackling crow or cooing wood pigeon, the bleating sheep, but no human voice other than Tryphena's and his own.

The poems Hardy wrote about Tryphena only began to appear in his books long after their affair ended. She'd married a pub owner named Charles Gale and moved with him to Topsham, in Devon, shortly before Hardy married Emma, and even though Tryphena was his cousin, they'd lost contact. News of her death in 1890, when she was thirty-nine and Hardy fifty, jarred him and triggered the writing of his final novel and several poems—a response he was to have again more than twenty-two years later, and to a much greater extent, when Emma died.

Tryphena, still young, appeared in his mind as she was "when her dreams were upbrimming with light." He made a pilgrimage to Coomb eweleaze and wrote a poem imagining a conversation in which she convinced him not to commit suicide lest no one be left alive to remember her. Once again, the actual Tryphena, the actual woman with her surviving husband and four children, had no present reality for him. He possessed no letters of hers, no keepsake, "no mark of her." She was a "phantom" retained in his mind, and now that she was gone from the world he gave this phantom final definition as his Lost Prize.

Beverly and I sat under one of the trees. As we talked about all this, I couldn't shake the image of Hardy, for days after hearing the news of Tryphena's death in early March, going into his Max Gate study and sitting at his desk, pen in hand, motionless as he considered what it meant to him. Yes, there were other women he'd fallen for. But as the rhymes gathered momentum in his brain ("lost prize" and "her eyes," "last days" and "sweet ways"), as the scaffolding of form began to assemble, as the usual process of control exerted itself, Hardy made himself see beyond all that. Losing Tryphena when they were young, a loss echoed and made utterly final now as he passed fifty, was the Great Loss, though it was a loss he had brought about and for which he was responsible. His other lost loves—his other losses of interest in his loves—were merely undulating waves emanating from this central loss. Aftershocks. In giving up on Tryphena, he had given up on the kind of love he most wanted to have, one whose power and reality endured.

He'd punished himself for that ever since. He'd pursued women who, by loving him, by accepting him as worthy of them, had thereby demonstrated their foolishness and unworthiness. In the harshest judgment of all, he'd married a woman he knew he could never love as he'd loved Tryphena. A woman for whom his love was already dampened. It was a specific Dantean torment that he believed, somewhere deep in his soul, he deserved.

There's a strange sketch Hardy drew for *Wessex Poems*, the book he published in 1898 that contained the poems about Tryphena. This sketch clearly demonstrates that he held himself accountable for losing his love all those years before. It captures Coomb eweleaze with its sheep, group of trees, hedge, stile. But suspended in the foreground, dominating everything, is a pair of large black-framed spectacles through which some of the landscape, particularly the trees, is visible. The remainder of the landscape can be seen above, below, and to the sides of the spectacle's frames. Critics suggest the sketch shows Hardy simultaneously viewing past and present through these lenses: the part seen through spectacles represents the aging man's perspective looking back at the past and the part outside the spectacles represents the way things look now. But Hardy has placed the spectacles with the temple pieces turned away from the viewer. The eweleaze is looking at him; he's not looking at it. In fact, he's refusing to see it as it is now, has removed his glasses to ensure that he isn't distracted, and opened himself to its scrutiny. To its judgment. The image insists that the past, and this place, and particularly the trees that create the most concealed spot in the leaze, have him in sharp view. Hardy, on his pilgrimage here after Tryphena's death, gazed at the place where his love and loss were greatest and found it looking back at him, watching him, seeing him clearly. Not letting him escape. It feels as though, when he put his spectacles back on, they held the leaze's vision of his guilt.

⇔

In July, four months after her death, Hardy knew the poems he'd written about Tryphena weren't enough to ease what he felt. He needed to go to her.

There was only one person he trusted enough to share the journey. Despite the heat, he convinced his brother Henry to accompany him by bicycle.

The trip from Dorchester to Topsham was more than sixty miles but they were used to long rides and could stay overnight at Lyme Regis if they felt tired. As it turned out, there was no need for that. They reached Topsham in late morning and purchased a small wreath.

At the cemetery Hardy stood beside his brother in silence, unable to pray, unwilling to recite a poem. There was welcome shade from a pair of old ash trees. He placed the wreath on Tryphena's still fresh-looking grave. Then he stood back and stared. Henry mumbled a few words about the Sparks family but stopped when he noticed Hardy moving away from him in order to avoid hearing what was being said.

Henry looked over at his brother and, seeing Hardy's features distorted as though melting, seeing him reach into his pocket for a handkerchief, decided to walk around the cemetery for a while and then wait by their bicycles.

"Home?" Henry asked when Hardy finally joined him.

Hardy had been thinking about just that question. Because as he stood by Tryphena's grave, as he tried to imagine going on after having witnessed its raw *thereness*, he realized he needed to visit Charles Gale too. Needed to see him and, even more urgently, needed to see Tryphena's children. See what they looked like, confront their living presence in the world. It would be necessary if he were ever to get his thoughts and feelings back under control. And to do that, he knew, he would have to write about them all. So it was essential to see them.

The brothers rode in silence to the Gales' home. Hardy knocked on the door. It was answered by Tryphena's eleven-year-old daughter, Nellie, who led them to the parlor and went to seek her father.

Gale was cutting bread and butter in the pantry and refused to join them. He told her to entertain them herself.

So Nellie served the bread and butter with slices of ham, kept their teacups full, and spoke with the Hardy brothers. She knew who Thomas Hardy was, had even read *Far from the Madding Crowd*. She felt something familiar in his presence, felt a tie, and so did the men. Her mother's cousins, and so her own.

In some respects, that told Hardy most of what he needed to know. He hadn't seen Tryphena in nearly twenty years, but he felt like he was with her again. He rose to go, tugging on his cap.

Outside, Henry said she looked so much like her mother. He bent to kiss her good-bye. Hardy said nothing. As they got on their bicycles, Charles Gale appeared in the courtyard, caught Hardy's eye, and nodded.

The sun was still bright. Hardy felt certain they could get home before dark.

⁂

Beverly and I passed a bottle of water back and forth as we watched a cloud's reflection drift over the leaze. We were both tired, a little drowsy. I felt ready to get home to Portland, though I also felt there was more to be done in Dorset, that Hardy and I hadn't quite finished our current business.

"When I think about Hardy marrying Emma," I said, "I can't help thinking about my father."

"How so?"

"Well, my father let the love of his life go too. Then he married a woman he didn't love and knew would make him miserable." The story felt so immediate to me that I began telling it in the present tense. "He accompanies his friend Simon, who's a heavyweight prize fighter, to serve as cornerman at a bout in New Jersey. That's when he meets a gentile woman who's the sister of Si's opponent. Her name, if I remember right, is Sally O'Day. She's in her brother's corner and my father can't take his eyes off her, forgets to give Si water between rounds, forgets to towel him off and tend his cuts. After the fight, he talks with Sally. My father's so in love he drives all the way from Brooklyn to Rahway to see this woman a couple times a week even though he has to be back in Brooklyn to open his chicken market before dawn. He proposes to her and brings her home to meet his deeply observant parents, my grandfather at the dinner table in his yarmulke, my grandmother saying the Sabbath prayers. Later, they tell him if he marries this *Shiksa*, they'll disown him. They'll sell the building where he rents his market space. And he caves. Let's the love of his life go." I was nearly breathless by then, and Beverly reached out to take both of my hands in hers. "And a year later he marries a woman who disdains him and his family and his work, a woman impossible for him to love."

We sat there listening to the dog in the distance. A plume of exhaust rose from the tractor at the far edge of the field and a few seconds later we heard the belch of its engine.

"But that story," Beverly said gently. "It's fiction. You made it up twenty years ago."

I turned to look at her. "I made it up?"

"When you were writing *The Open Door*."

When she said that, the memory flooded back. Shortly after I moved to the woods and we married, I'd begun working on a memoir about living with brain damage. Part of it, seeking to establish continuity with the person I'd been before getting sick, explored what I recalled or could research about my childhood. But I felt stymied by a few central questions: How did my parents meet and why did these two people, who hated each other so violently that their mutual rage turned on their two sons, marry? And stay married? At the time I was doing this, my mother was suffering from dementia and my father's siblings were either very aged or dead. There was no one to answer my questions and nothing I was able to discover beyond my aunt Evelyn's comment: "He married your mother on the rebound." I felt stuck in the memoir, where I wouldn't allow myself to include anything that wasn't verifiable and true but where I needed to understand the forces at work. So I decided to set aside my memoir and write a novel that addressed my questions. I needed to make up a story that felt true to what I knew about my parents. Like an actor imagining a backstory for his character that informs what he shows on stage, but is never revealed, my fiction would permit me to return to my memoir without including the story of their courtship. I would know what I needed to know in order to continue.

Apparently, over the subsequent two decades, I'd internalized the fictional story. I'd given readings that included the lost-love part of my novel, been interviewed about it, and memory had consolidated the narrative as true. I believed that my father, after failing to stand up for his love, had married my mother in the wake of losing Sally O'Day. It was an act of self-punishment similar to the one Thomas Hardy had performed, and having read so much by and about Hardy over the years, I must have unconsciously had his sad story in mind when I wrote *The Open Door*.

⸎

We snuggled together on the blanket and were tired enough to fall asleep right away. We couldn't have moved if we'd wanted to.

Thomas Hardy walked along a narrow curvy road I hadn't noticed bisecting the leaze. He wore a gray crown-shaped straw hat glinting with sunlight, and his jacket, pants, and shoes were all gray. A woman walked beside him, draped in reddish brown. Though stocky, she seemed insubstantial, not as fully materialized as the garments she wore. The couple came toward us but overhanging trees screened their view.

Then I heard an engine shift gears. A large vehicle, perhaps a tractor or combine harvester, was approaching but couldn't be seen because of a deep dip in the road. Hardy and his companion were oblivious. I tried to signal him about the danger ahead, but was immobilized where I lay.

The vehicle rose into view. I saw now it was the kind of enormous rig the British call an articulated lorry. Inside the cab sat a figure who initially reminded me of my father. I don't know why, because he looked nothing like my father—wasn't round-faced and jut-jawed and bald, didn't have a cigar jammed between his lips, wasn't wearing eyeglasses.

Then he waved, lifting both hands from the steering wheel in a flying gesture I recognized at once. I saw his hair flaring wildly, his shoulders covered in ash. The driver was Robert Russell, ancient-looking and no longer blind. Alive. I turned away and saw that Hardy and the woman were stilled, freeze-framed. They were perfectly balanced in midstride, smiling, but going nowhere. I looked back and saw the lorry also motionless, neither advancing up the incline nor sliding back down, its nose pointed heavenward. Russell beckoned. Though Beverly and I remained where we were, we also were beside him. He leaned out of the window and smiled. On the side of the lorry was a sign bearing the cover image of Russell's book *To Catch an Angel*.

"It's good to be back in England," he said. "I didn't see much of it the last time I was here."

"When you and Elizabeth met," I said.

"We were happy together for the next fifty-five years." Russell smiled at us. "Speaking of which: You found out, didn't you?"

"I always knew you and Elizabeth were happy together."

"That's not what I meant." He looked at me and then at Beverly. "The last time we spoke, you asked what I thought Hardy would have made of your happiness together with Beverly. Remember what I said?"

Of course! He said that Hardy would tell me eventually.

Russell, leaning back in the driver's seat that had transformed into his old office chair, followed my thoughts.

"And he did tell you, didn't he?"

"The ponies," Beverly whispered, waking me from my dream. "I just dreamt about the ponies."

"I think I did too."

I pulled her even closer to me. I could feel her breath in my ear as she said, "I realized something the moment I woke up: When the ponies came to us at the pond, it was a Visitation, wasn't it? A real visitation."

⸙

When I was first engaged with Hardy's novels in 1968, Russell didn't want me to read biographical or critical work. A committed advocate of New Criticism, he'd taught me the merit of engaging directly and exclusively with the text, and trained me in close reading. But I cheated a little. I found a used one-volume edition of the self-ghostwritten biography, *The Life of Thomas Hardy*. Reading around in it, I encountered a scene I've never forgotten in which Hardy describes himself as frenzied by creative inspiration. He says he composes sometimes indoors, sometimes out, and on occasion finds himself without a scrap of paper at the very moment that he feels volumes. So he would write on large dead leaves, white chips left by the wood-cutters, or pieces of stone or slate that came to hand.

It was the fall of 1873 and Hardy was thirty-three. Since Tryphena had moved to London, and Hardy had become engaged to Emma despite her parents' humiliating rejection of him, he'd written three novels in three years. Now he was writing his fourth, *Far from the Madding Crowd*, at home in Bockhampton, and getting paid well for its serial publication. The book would even appear in America. Hardy finally knew exactly what he was doing as a fiction writer. He'd listened well to critics of his first books and to friends, had developed his Dorset literary landscape and characters, found his subject in love's geometry. Working in seclusion from his fiancée in Cornwall and from his London connections, it had all come together for him.

This elated, fevered writer in the grip of inspiration, this scrawler on dead leaves and wood chips and stone was not the coolly withdrawn, calculating, self-controlled maker of carefully crafted fiction and poetry that the conventional Hardy image had established. I think that reading about Hardy like this, at that time in my life, was when I began to see and love him, when the screen of the books parted and the unguarded man looked out at me with wild ecstatic eyes. Hardy scribbling on a stone is the Hardy I carry in my heart. And he's the essential Hardy, I feel, very much like the Hardy in love with Tryphena rather than the Hardy withdrawn from Emma or prosy and formal with Florence.

This may be why *Far from the Madding Crowd* is his novel that captivates me the most. It doesn't move me like *Two on a Tower* does, or impress me with its gravity like *The Mayor of Casterbridge*, or horrify me like *Jude the Obscure*. But it enthralls me. It's funny, romantic, tragic, full of credible life and dramatic scenes. The flawed characters and their great passions hold my unwavering attention. I look for passages that feel as though they'd been written on leaves in Hardy's sudden delirium. "The sky was clear—remarkably clear—and the twinkling of all the stars seemed to be but throbs of one body, timed by a common pulse." As I read the novel, I remain aware that *Far from the Madding Crowd* was the book that changed Hardy's life. For one thing, its financial success enabled Hardy finally to marry Emma, or rather removed his last honorable excuse for delay. It brought him into the mainstream of literary life, particularly London literary life, and provided an opportunity to meet fascinating men and women unlike those he'd known in Dorset or Cornwall or even in his previous times in London. Leslie

Stephen, Virginia Woolf's father, became Hardy's magazine publisher, advisor, and confidante. Edmund Gosse, the poet, critic, and author of the classic autobiography *Father and Son*, became a close lifelong friend.

The success of *Far from the Madding Crowd* also introduced Hardy to Helen Paterson, who would illustrate the published novel and, during a few crucial months shortly before his marriage, steal Hardy's heart. Helen was young, twenty-five, charming and attractive, an artist, and she was receptive to Hardy's interest in providing her with sketches of Dorset or of farm implements and structures to assist in her work. They dined together, sometimes with friends, sometimes alone, and he kept coming up with suggestions for further meetings. She should see how a piper stood when he played at a sheep-shearing supper, or how the authentic supper table was laid and what a smock frock or sheepcrook looked like. What kind of birds would fly by. The howling dog, the snowball, gaiters, Sergeant Troy's sword. When Helen married the poet William Allingham in the summer, Hardy was bereft. Though he was set to marry Emma the next month, he thought with regret—well into old age—that Helen was the woman he should have married "but for a stupid blunder of God Almighty and the bitter workings of the tide of chance."

In this frame of mind, and after a four-year engagement, Thomas Hardy and Emma Gifford were wed. If Hardy ever wrote or spoke about the wedding itself, nothing of it survived. Emma recalled that the day they were married was "a perfect September day—the 17th, 1874—not brilliant sunshine, but wearing a soft, sunny luminousness; just as it should be."

I read that brief description and mourn for them both. The moment seems full of decline: summer about to become fall, the brilliant sunshine and bright hopes of a time more full of light and dreams have peaked. And this duller light seems just as it should be.

14

So, any Hardy sightings today?" Anthony and Nan were in the dining room when we arrived, just as they'd been yesterday.

"Oh please, Anthony," Nan said. She stood and turned toward us, raising her eyebrows in apology. "Tea for you both this afternoon? I picked up some gluten-free soy milk this morning."

"That sounds perfect," Beverly told her.

We sat across from Anthony and before I could stop myself I said, "More than a sighting." Then I described what had happened in the Nut Walk at Max Gate. When I was done, I felt equally relieved and embarrassed. Well, we'd make a good story at the next meeting of the Dorset B&B Association, if there was such a thing.

"Would you tell me again what Hardy said?" Anthony's expression seemed like a mix of confusion and concern.

"Nothing is as you wish it."

"I see."

Nan returned with our tea. As she served us, Anthony kept adjusting the position of his cup and saucer, folding and refolding his napkin, frowning.

"Does Hardy's statement mean anything to you?" I asked him.

"Let me ask if you've read *The Mayor of Casterbridge*."

"Three times. Though not for a while. Plus we saw a made-for-TV version eight or nine years ago. Ciarán Hinds played the Mayor."

"Yes. Of course. And if I remember correctly, you felt Hardy first touch and talk to you outside the Mayor's house?"

"Right. Yesterday morning, roughly the same hour as when he showed up today."

"I don't know quite what to make of this, you see. But 'nothing is as you wish it' is a direct quote from *The Mayor of Casterbridge*. My son has that very sentence hanging on a bulletin board in his office. Along with other cheerful and self-encouraging messages."

"That's . . . I . . . You're sure?"

"It's quite a memorable scene in the novel. Susan Henchard is dying and reveals a few secrets to her daughter while concealing others. Very Hardy, that. Conceal under the guise of a massive reveal. Susan's scheme to find Elizabeth-Jane a good husband has failed. She wishes she could be around to see things work out, but she's learned that in life nothing is as you wish it."

Nan got up and walked to the bookcase against the dining room's far wall. She brought back a copy of *The Mayor of Casterbridge* and handed it to Anthony. As he leafed through the pages, he said, "In the end, ironically enough, Elizabeth-Jane does marry well. The very man her mother schemed for. She also finds out the truth of her parentage, which ends in reconciliation with her real father."

"So everything was as wished for," Beverly said.

"Much of it was, yes. For some of the ladies in the story, anyway. The Mayor himself, no. Dies in proper Hardy manner: broken, alone, dishonored by his own basest instincts."

"I don't know what to think," I said.

"Here it is," Anthony muttered, handing over the book. "Underlined in #2 pencil, no doubt by my son. Page 111."

I didn't need to read it. In fact, I could hardly focus on the words before me, which I would never forget. But which, apparently, I had already not forgotten even though I hadn't remembered them. But won't forget again:

"I wish it could have been in my time! But there—nothing is as you wish it."

All of us have experienced moments when memory is inaccessible. When the effort to remember isn't enough to produce the memory being sought. You enter a room and can't recall what you're there for. You can't find the car keys in the green ceramic dish by the front door where you always leave them, so you search and search the house, then in frustration thrust your hands in your pockets and there are the keys. A friend's name, the country where they had that tsunami, the stadium where the Dodgers played, your daughter's new phone number. It's on the tip of your tongue, you think, all you need is a moment and it'll come to you. That adjective you know isn't "affordable" but sounds like "affordable" and means how delightful and lovable and charming your wife looks: You look so affordable, dear, when you mean to say she looks, um, looks, looks: *Adorable!* Wide receivers forget routes they've practiced over and over; actors forget lines they know cold.

We all have also experienced the moment when a remark someone makes, or an image seen, a scent, a sound triggers memory. Your brother sings a phrase from "Party Doll," Buddy Knox's big hit song that topped the charts for a week in March 1957, when you were almost ten, and suddenly it's all there right before your eyes: the room you shared with him, the beds side-by-side with a single-drawer walnut table between them, your posters of the planets and the dinosaurs and the flags of the nations, your red toy chest and his puny scarred desk next to the window that opened onto a view of sooty brick. All of that was lost in memory, was stranded in some isolated cranny of cellular material waiting to be sparked.

It's rarer to find yourself quoting lines without recognizing them as such, without knowing you were remembering them. Without an inkling, even after you hear them. My mind knew the lines from this novel I'd read three times, and knew they were associated with Thomas Hardy. But I didn't. And realizing that this is what must have happened made me feel a kind of alienation from myself, a lack of integration with my own mind that I've felt often in the years since the viral attack on my brain. It's much less common now, after two dozen years, because I'm more adept at being brain damaged. I've learned to manage my symptoms, and to live with them when they can't be managed, and not be stymied. I've learned how to embed important memories, or at least to give them the best chance of being retained. To accommodate the essentially fragmented way my memory now works. But every once in a while, something like this happens, or like my false memory of my father's romance, and I'm reminded of how deceptive the command of memory can be. Reminded of the peculiarities of my neurological workings and their phenomena, their electrical disturbances.

I'm frequently in the process of discovering what I already know. Of suddenly remembering what I've lost but have not forgotten and could not—cannot—have retrieved by will. Like all of us, even those who don't know it's true, my life is an ongoing mystery to me. Oh, maybe more of a mystery because the clues are so easily missed or lost. But that's only a matter of degree, isn't it? Sometimes the most fruitful way for me to discover what's hidden in my life is to look away, look at other people's lives without intending to explore my own. To make room for discovery. And, it would seem, for Visitations.

"There's a little more to tell you," I said, and explained about the ponies at Rushy Pond.

"Our heath-croppers," Nan said. "Lovely animals. Four of them there, I believe. Dartmoor ponies, they are. Reintroduced last year, keep the scrub from growing back after the rangers removed it all."

"But you saw more in them than that," Anthony whispered, "as I believe you're saying. As I saw Sir Francis Drake and company in the waves of the South Atlantic."

"I thought of your experience as we were walking back through the woods," I said. "Thank you."

"Something else just occurred to me," Anthony said. "Both of Hardy's statements to you sound quite alike, don't they? 'Something I missed' and 'Nothing is as you wish it.' That *miss* and *wish*, or rather *missed* and *wish it*."

"They sound like the wind," Nan said, looking down into her cup. "The hissing sound that makes us use words like 'whish' or 'swish' or 'whisper' to describe it."

I thought about the two times Hardy had spoken to me. Both were accompanied by a surge of wind. On South Street before the Mayor's house in Dorchester I had thought at first the voice was actually the wind in my ear. At Max Gate, an odd breeze at the mouth of the Nut Walk was strong enough to make my eyes water and it intensified just as Hardy spoke. Had that been all it was? A trick of the mind, an electrical firing among damaged neurons that was brought on by shifting, whishing, whispering wind?

⇒

All that was clear to me was that I needed a break, some serious free time before the play tonight. Both of us did. Since we'd already had our long walk for the day and had napped, we decided to spend an hour relaxing in our room.

Beverly ran a bath and I sat in the easy chair by our bed catching up on e-mail and news from the Internet. Bill Clinton had appeared on a New York stage with President Obama yesterday, raising campaign money and showing solidarity. The last transit of Venus in the twenty-first century would occur tonight, Scotland beat Australia in rugby, Kenny G. turned fifty-six. A Thanksgiving service was held at St. Paul's Cathedral for the Queen's Diamond Jubilee followed by lunch in Westminster Hall and a formal carriage procession to Buckingham Palace. Our house sitter texted us a photo of our cat Max lying on his back in a streak of sunlight and told us he was looking forward to seeing us soon.

I closed the laptop and gazed out the window. Tired but not drowsy, trying to clear my mind, I listened to the occasional lapping of bathwater that told me Beverly had lain back and was getting comfortable. Within that sound I became aware of another sound, a soft scratching like tree branches just barely in contact with a window.

No, it was like the sound of a pen moving across paper. Moving quickly, then more steadily, then not at all. Now quickly again. There was faint murmuring too, a voice that wasn't Beverly's. I was in the bedroom at the B&B, but I was also not. I was in Max Gate. In Hardy's final study, the one he used during the last thirty years of his working life. I recognized the layout, the fireplace with its familiar tiles and array of pictures above the mantel, small rectangular rug, wicker trash basket, packed bookshelves, and the table in the middle of the room piled with still more books. A fiddle leaned against the corner of one bookcase and a cello was balanced against a wall.

And Thomas Hardy sat writing at the large desk by the window. The glow from his lamp sharpened the scene. Though it was late afternoon and warm, he wore a dress shirt with a high stand collar and black cravat, a dark coat and vest.

Papers sprawled across the desk's surface, some facing sideways, some upside down, many dense with crossed-out passages and marginal additions. Some were yellowed, some curled like leaves and showing script on both sides of the page. None of the pages looked as though they'd been typed. Hardy normally was a contained writer, his manuscripts—even their cross-outs—tidy as an architect's drawing. I knew that he preferred to write amid neatness and order, in space as well dressed as he was, always controlled, steady. Something else was happening here.

I was directly behind Hardy as he scrawled. This was the first time I'd ever had a Visitation in which I did the Visiting. In which I left my home setting. How long would it last? I tried to steady my breathing, slow my racing heartbeat. I didn't know if Hardy knew I was there, but I didn't believe so and didn't want to interrupt him. I felt the need to go slow, to notice everything I could. To remember. Because, I understood, this would be my last Visitation with Hardy. This was it, this was my chance to find out what I needed to know.

Hardy sighed and bent closer to the paper before him. He was mostly bald, mostly gray where he did have hair, beardless but with a dapper gray moustache, its tips carefully twisted. This was Hardy, circa

1900. A sixty-year-old man possessed by his work, fraught and struggling in the act of composition.

He wrote in bursts, sometimes raising his pen off the page entirely and tapping its top against his teeth as he stared out the window. To his left, rising from the clutter, was a thick stack of manuscript paper, the pages face down, haphazardly aligned. Hardy lifted the top page off the stack—which would have been the last page he'd placed there—and began reading it. He looked up at the view through his window, then back down at the page and spoke a line aloud: "Saddened even as he felt such joy, Patrick Stone lay with his dearest rue under a canopy of bird song." Satisfied, Hardy put it back and began writing again.

Given its layout on the pages, and the unmetered and unrhymed sentence I'd heard him read, Hardy was engaged in a work of prose, not poetry. Obviously a novel. A very substantial novel that looked to have been in progress for many years.

Hardy abruptly stood. I was afraid he might somehow have detected my presence. Did a Visitor give off shadows? Could I be seen reflected in his window? I could see his reflection there, but where mine should be I saw only the wall behind me.

Hardy took off his coat and vest and flung them on top of a cabinet beside him. He opened his collar, yanked off his cravat. His movements looked desperate, like those of a man struggling to catch his breath. Then I heard a sob, and a series of deep inhalations.

Like a man surrendering, Hardy sank back down. He opened his desk drawer, took out a page of sketches and studied it. There were faces drawn in his expert manner, quick and deft, a man and woman. The man was recognizably Hardy as a young man and below his image was the word *Stone*. The woman resembled the photograph Beverly had shown me earlier that day: Tryphena Sparks. Below her image was the word *Heart*. Hardy studied them for maybe thirty seconds, though the time felt endless.

Then he put the sketches away, shut the drawer, and picked up his pen. He continued writing as I approached the desk and stood behind him. I could see the new sentences as they were created: "That week

Patrick Stone and Ruby Heartsfield met by the crooked tree at the edge of the leaze every afternoon at the same hour. He had not known such happiness was possible. Nor such elation. His Ruby. His Rue."

I felt certain Hardy was writing a scene set in the place where Beverly and I had just been, Coomb eweleaze. It was a scene between Hardy and Tryphena, loosely disguised. He shook his head, crossed out "He had not known such happiness was possible," and scrawled, "He had always hoped such happiness was possible." Then he slashed his pen through that line and wrote, "He had known such happiness was possible but had not dared to risk seizing it."

With the same ferocity, he revised the rest of the passage. He was working, I knew, to make it as honest and true as he could. When he paused, I reread the lines: "That week Patrick Stone and Ruby Heartsfield met by the crooked tree at the edge of the leaze every afternoon at the same hour. He had known such happiness was possible but had not dared to risk seizing it. Nor had he dared such ecstasy, lest losing it later destroy him. What a fool he had been. What a fool he still could be. His Ruby. His Rue."

The page now complete, Hardy added it to the stack, which he then lifted, turned face up, straightened, and placed back on his desk. I could read the title page:

Something I Missed:
A Novel of Love
Found and Lost
and Mourned
By
Thomas Hardy

He was, it seemed, at the end of his day's work. He stood, but didn't turn around to leave. Instead, he reached into his drawer again. He withdrew the sketches and lifted the page to his lips.

And then I was no longer at Max Gate. There was no fade, no final glimpse of the man or his study. I was just comfortably in the easy chair by the bed in our B&B and could hear Beverly's bathwater begin to drain. She was singing from an old English folk song, "the water is wide, I can't cross over," and I knew I was back where I needed to be for good.

⁂

Was it possible? Had Thomas Hardy, long after he supposedly quit writing novels, written one called "Something I Missed," which he never published?

To my knowledge, the story of Hardy's split career has never been doubted. Novels for twenty-eight years / no novels for the next thirty-three years.

Disgusted by the outpouring of brutal and often personal criticism over *Tess of the D'Urbervilles* in 1891 and *Jude the Obscure* in 1895, Hardy claimed that the experience completely cured him of further interest in novel writing. The reaction to his work, he said, compelled him, "if he wished to retain any shadow of self-respect, to abandon at once a form of literary art he had long intended to abandon at some indefinite time." He would henceforth focus only on poetry. Writing novels, he insisted, was something he'd done for money, and—ironically—after the scandalous, controversial reception of his last novels he had money aplenty. Those novels, which he said were the least important half of his work from a purely literary standpoint, were not where he practiced true art. That was in the poetry, the higher calling, and poetry was all he would write in the future.

Some biographers and critics have suggested that there was more to the decision than Hardy merely reacting to his critics. They noted that he'd reached the point where, as Martin Seymour-Smith put it, "he was now finding prose no longer adequate for what he wished to say and was writing more poems" anyway. Robert Gittings thought "the highly personal themes of his secret youth were now beginning to force themselves uncomfortably into his novels. . . . When he attached them to a novelist's human characters, they became too self-revealing. Poems could reveal more of the emotion, but less of the biographical circumstances." Claire Tomalin viewed it as a savvy career move, "a dramatic gesture from a novelist at the pinnacle of success, controversial but hugely admired, translated, discussed all over the Western world and rich from his royalties."

So they all saw additional motives, but never doubted that Hardy had, indeed, quit writing novels.

But, my God, what if he hadn't? What if Thomas Hardy had secretly written another novel and never published it, never let anyone know he was doing it, never even risked having it typed? A novel written out of such personal urgency and so revealing, so true about his life, that—if he even could finish it—Hardy destroyed it. Or hid it.

⚜

While Beverly dried her hair, I thought about what Hardy might have done with "Something I Missed." That is, if it ever existed.

Knowing what I did about him, I couldn't imagine he'd actually destroy it. Not this manuscript. He'd burned so much, but this, I felt, would be different. This seemed like a book written to assuage decades of guilt and sadness, to understand and atone for what he'd destroyed once already. He couldn't destroy it again.

If he'd hidden the manuscript, and it hadn't been found by Florence when she executed the terms of Hardy's will and gave his things to the Dorset County Museum, or in the process of various Max Gate remodelings and rehabilitations, or by the many tenants who'd lived there before it became a tourist site, or by the swarms of visitors, I thought it might be hidden someplace other than Max Gate. And therefore nearly impossible to find. There were too many possibilities: The cottage at Bockhampton? The heath? A site associated with Tryphena—in Puddletown or Weymouth or Topsham or buried somewhere in Coomb eweleaze? In London?

This wasn't something I could envision discussing with anyone other than Beverly. Not even with Anthony and Nan, who knew about my Visitations. Nor was I going to start hunting for "Something I Missed." It was just too crazy. If Hardy wanted me to know where it was now, he would show me.

When I told Beverly about my Visitation she said the existence of a secret Hardy novel sounded so plausible that it was surprising rumors about it weren't already in circulation. A cache of unknown work, à la J. D. Salinger. She also mentioned that a ruby was a talisman of passion. And that, in addition to its connotations of regret and loss, the word *Rue* also referred to an herb that, when chewed, was known to ease the wild beating of a heart. It soothed. It improved vision. It warded off witches' spells.

⏛

I showered and we went for a drive. If some time on British roads didn't clear my head, nothing would. There was a pub that would cater to our diet located about a dozen miles east in Church Knowle, and on the way we listened to a call-in show. Sir Elton John's performance at last night's Jubilee concert was rubbish, Sir Paul McCartney should let the younger performers have their day, Sir Tom Jones was over. It was all too safe and Sir-ish. And not everyone in the country approved of the celebrations or of the monarchy, either. Waste of money. Country's gone to pot, all the foreigners and all.

The pub was busy and loud, just what we needed, and the fish was fresh. Nobody was talking about Thomas Hardy.

Heading back to the B&B, we followed the road through the Lulworth Firing Range that we'd noticed yesterday. The range was a Ministry of Defense zone normally closed to all traffic and used for training at the Armored Fighting Vehicles Gunnery School. They shoot live shells in there. But in honor of the Jubilee holidays the shooting was halted and the road opened, though few tourists seemed to know. We had it to ourselves except for the occasional tank hulks scattered on the landscape. And for the sheep. As I came out of a blind curve a dozen of them were spread across the road. I braked and had to laugh, thinking that after all the nightmare-inducing narrow overhung shadowy roads with their concealed hazards and speeding onrushing dangers, it would be a perfect cartoon ending for a flock of sheep to be the thing that finally caused me to crash or our tire to explode. Still, the view was astounding on this ancient ridge road, a clear panoramic line of sight to Dorset's Jurassic Coast. Beverly got out her camera and took some landscape photos to use as inspiration for her painting after we got home.

Anthony and Nan were waiting when we returned. He'd offered to walk us to the makeshift theater and be sure we got good seats, and since the other three guests had already checked in, Nan joined us.

"Don't forget to bring jackets along. Gets cold there by the cove, come evening."

⏚

It was just a quarter mile down Main Road, but the walk took longer than we anticipated because we kept having to stand aside for passing cars. As we descended into the bowl of Lulworth Cove, about forty or fifty people had gathered.

"Look there," Nan whispered. "Dear me."

"Don't worry," Anthony replied. "This could be entertaining."

I thought they were talking about the man in long flowing white hair and an overcoat who stood by the side of the road declaiming Hardy's poem "At Lulworth Cove a Century Back." Around his neck hung a sign with the word *Time* printed on one side in heavy black ink. The word *Hardy* was printed on the other side. He flipped the sign to indicate whether it was Time or Hardy speaking particular lines in this elegy for the young John Keats, whose final steps on English soil were taken right here at Lulworth Cove. But the man had trouble projecting over the same trio we'd seen yesterday playing old-time reels and jigs in the parking lot. Now the hubbub of the gathering audience was adding to his problems. He was looking downcast. But maybe this was due to the poem itself. "That man goes to Rome—to death, despair."

Watching and listening to him as we walked, Beverly and I nearly bumped into Sharon Taylor. She'd been the target of Anthony and Nan's hushed exchange, and though she couldn't have overheard she greeted them without any of the warmth we'd seen in her yesterday. I wasn't sure she recognized us. But then she shifted her gaze in our direction and smiled.

"My gluten-free, Hardy-loving Americans," she said, grabbing Beverly's hands and shaking them. "I see we didn't poison you after all."

"We feel so lucky to be in Dorset on a show night. Just happened to hear about it today from the caretaker at Max Gate."

"And speaking of the devil," Sharon said as Jason stomped down the path behind us.

"Made it, I see!" He patted me on the back. "Hope it's worth your time. Hello, Ms. Taylor. Know they had to cast a new Sergeant Troy only three days ago?"

"I hadn't heard about that," Sharon said. "What happened to Laurence White?"

"Actually got a small part in *Game of Thrones*. Agent phoned up. Two episodes. Fill in for someone. Be on set in Morocco by yesterday."

"What lovely news for Laurence."

"Who replaced him?" Nan asked.

"That's another unfortunate bit. Edgar Ellis."

"I see. Had to redo the costumes, did they?"

Anthony turned to us and said, "Edgar, bless him, is quite a bit shorter and let us say bulkier than Laurence (Don't-Call-Me-Larry) White."

"Awkward, that, what with Serena Mulry being six foot tall," Sharon said. "Her height worked well next to Laurence, no doubt. And I believe there was also an extra, well, an extra connection between Serena and Laurence as things went on."

"Sharon, really," Anthony said. "Nothing but gossip. Serena has been with Alison Patel for years now. You know that."

The music stopped and we all headed toward the stage at the center of the parking lot. Folding chairs were set out in ten neat rows of about thirty each. The meadow where we'd seen the cast rehearsing was off to the right. To the left of the stage stood a crowd of actors in costume trying to be inconspicuous beside some small trees and shrubbery. It seemed as though almost all of the sparse audience were local people and they exchanged greetings for a couple of minutes. We had no trouble finding seats all together and close to the stage. There was a sharp whistle from behind us. Jason turned and put up his hand in response. Katie Pole Crosbie, the caretaker of Hardy's cottage, joined us. She and Jason embraced, and he whispered something in her ear. She nodded and kissed his neck. I noticed that he didn't reach for his hand sanitizer. Once the audience had settled, the director—still carrying his fiddle—strode to center stage.

"On behalf of the Hardy Theatre Company, welcome, friends, to the partly real, partly dream-country of Dorset's late great poet and novelist. I'm Geoffrey Mills. Tonight's performance will be a partly real, partly dream-adaptation of *Far from the Madding Crowd*. It will pay particular attention to matters of the heart, or The Geometry of Love as our young advisor, scholar, and script-rescuer Jason Abbott calls it. Jason? Stand up please and let us see you."

Jason rose an inch, waved, and said, "No, no. No need. No need, no."

"We make no claim to be telling the whole story or adhering to its local geography. There will be six scenes," the director continued. "And, all going well, no intermission."

This made everyone except me and Beverly erupt in prolonged laughter. Anthony leaned across Nan and tried to explain to us why it was so funny. Around a series of noises I understood to be chuckles, he said the performances of *Far from the Madding Crowd* were being held here in the parking lot on a makeshift stage because the stage at their usual venue—Max Gate—had collapsed midway through closing night of their previous production, *The Woodlanders*, forcing a forty-minute intermission in which the set and all the props were moved onto the lawn before the play could continue. Indeed, this week's performances were rushed into production as a fundraising enterprise to build a more durable and portable stage.

The director thanked us for attending and left the audience in a giddy mood. He rejoined his fellow musicians at the side of the stage and they began to play one of Hardy's favorite airs from childhood, "My Fancy-Lad." After a minute had passed, a bearded young man built like a fullback and wearing shapeless old corduroys with a matching cap strode onstage. He carried a shepherd's crook.

After the play, the seven of us went to a pub across the street from the parking lot. It was located in a sixteenth-century thatched inn, with seats outdoors that overlooked the cove. Dogs wound their way around and between tables, happy, nuzzling for handouts.

Anthony and Jason ordered Star Gazer ales with plates of chips and mushy peas and olives for the table. Nan touted their cask beer and Sharon recommended the medium-sweet Dorset cider, which was gluten-free, but we stuck with red wine and Katie with a single malt scotch from the Isle of Skye.

We all agreed that Gabriel Oak's dowsing of the straw rick fire was the play's most exciting scene. And the burial of Fanny Robin with her stillborn child was the most moving. All the actors did well.

"Bathsheba," Jason said. "Superb. Showed that she loved each of her three men differently. Held something back as well. Serena got the angles right."

"A toast! To Love's Geometry," Katie said, and smiled at Jason.

"So embarrassing," Jason sighed, blushing. "I do wish Geoffrey hadn't done that."

"Well then, to Thomas Hardy!" Anthony raised his glass. When beer sloshed onto his wrist, he laughed and said, "Oops-a-daisy, just like our Sergeant Troy."

"He spilled his beer the same way yesterday," Beverly said. "We happened to walk by during rehearsal."

That prompted Sharon to ask where we'd gone since she'd seen us for lunch. As we recounted our travels in Hardy country, Anthony watched and listened closely to see how much we'd reveal. I told about Max Gate, from the dining room to the attic to the Nut Walk and the Pet Cemetery, and about Durdle Door, about seeing heath-ponies at Rushy Pond and resting in Coomb eweleaze. But I didn't mention Visitations or investigations or phantom sources. Nor anything about Hardy's love life.

But I didn't have to. Our itinerary gave us away.

"Ahhh," Sharon said. "The Tryphena Pilgrimage."

"Now Sharon," Nan said. "No need to get started."

"If I may," Jason said. "By your logic, Sharon, they were on the Emma Pilgrimage too. Spent hours at Max Gate, after all. Lingered in Emma's attic room. Pet Cemetery." He looked at us and said, "You've been to Cornwall too?"

"Yes," Beverly said. "Four days last week. But we didn't visit any places connected with Emma or Hardy."

"Doesn't matter. Circumstantial evidence lets us conclude you were definitely on the Emma Pilgrimage."

"And don't forget they visited Hardy's cottage," Katie said. "Surely they were on the Pole Pilgrimage as well."

Undeterred, Sharon said, "I don't see what the big deal is. Don't get me wrong, I love the man's work. But people have known for more than eighty years that our placid old Thomas Hardy had much to hide. Bonfires in the garden and all. What does that tell you? And for fifty of those years they've known precisely what he had to hide. It's all in the poems, if you know what to look for. Hardy acolytes just didn't want to admit the incest, the secret child, the shameful cover-up. It's a totally credible story."

"As long as you don't concern yourself with evidence," Anthony said. "The slightest shred of proof or corroboration. Verification. Official papers. No, it's all based on the ravings of an aged woman with dementia who was being led on by a, you'll forgive me Sharon, Hardy wacko."

"Hardy destroyed the proof."

"All of it? And silenced all of Dorset in his own time? Somehow purged the official record?" Anthony took a drink of ale. "Let me tell you, for the benefit of our American guests, a far more credible story: Nothing happened between Thomas Hardy and Tryphena Sparks. She was sixteen and his cousin. A girl who'd been a child all Hardy's life."

Sharon tried to interrupt but Anthony held up his hand. "Let me finish. I know cousins could marry. I know girls married quite young. Hardy was ill, lonely, at loose ends. He visited her family in their time of troubles. This does not constitute grounds to assume an affair, Sharon, or any of the other rot that follows from that assumption. Because it's nothing more than that: a series of assumptions."

"There's a middle ground, is there not?" Jason said. "More credible still. Had a romance of some kind. Anything from a brief fling to full-on engagement. Broke up. Meant a little or meant a lot. Either way, world didn't end when they parted."

"As happened with Hardy over and over," said Katie. "Often simultaneously."

"Hardy became famous. Gossip followed." Jason grabbed a couple of olives and popped them in his mouth. "Pattern of behavior, you know. In his affairs just as clearly as in his novels. Needed to be involved with two or even three at once. Could never choose."

"You know," Beverly said, "sometimes it's hard not to be repelled by Hardy's pattern of behavior. As an adult he seems to be interested in a woman only to the extent that she listens to him and adores him. What he's after is an audience. Or a staff assistant. It's shallow. He's not there for the women he supposedly loves. Not until they die and he can perform his grieving act."

"Agreed," Katie said. "He suffered because of it, but so did Emma. So did Cassie. All his other quote unquote Beloveds."

Sharon had been jotting notes on her paper napkin. When the talk stopped, she looked around the table and smiled. "One thing I will say that can't be argued. Hardy is good for business."

"Hear, hear!" Nan said.

"It's a bit of a drive back to Wareham. I'd better go." Sharon stood and we all got up with her. She took one of my hands and one of Beverly's and held us for a moment. "It was lovely to see you again. I feel you'll be back with us in the future too. Don't forget Tea Is for Tess."

After she'd left, conversation drifted to other topics. Cool weather. Relief that the Jubilee holiday was almost over. The 2012 Olympic Games beginning next month in London. But my thoughts remained on Hardy. On "Something I Missed" and all this discussion of Hardy's loves, what was known and what was not.

I looked out over Lulworth Cove and thought about the scene in *Far from the Madding Crowd* where Sergeant Troy plunged into the sea right there at the cove's center where the water was calm. Disgusted with the tedium of farm life, gloomy over the death of his beloved Fanny Robin, disliking the company of his wife Bathsheba, Troy sought escape. How many times, I thought, Thomas Hardy must have had that fantasy. How many ways he imagined escaping from the torment that love was for him. He could not. Neither could Sergeant Troy, though he survived his swim, rescued by passing seamen and serving aboard their ship for a few months before returning to Dorset and his death at the hands of one of Bathsheba's thwarted suitors. Edgar Ellis, playing Troy, had resisted theatrics and used a simple tightening of his voice to convey his character's desperation. It worked, and it reminded me of Hardy's desperate efforts at control. Of himself. Of his story. Of his world. His effort to make them all cohere. My travels in Hardy country these last two days have helped me recognize how hard he worked at that.

I could imagine him as I'd seen him just a few hours earlier, driven nearly wild at his desk by an urgent need to reveal the truth, writing at the thin edge of control. I understood what he meant by saying "Something I missed." What I'd seen felt like the deepest truth I could know.

15

The next morning, before leaving Dorset for Heathrow Airport, we visited Thomas Hardy's grave at the St. Michael's churchyard in Stinsford. Hardy and his family worshipped in this church, played in the choir here, even helped restore the thirteenth-century building. We sat on a bench before the family's graves and looked at his memorial stone, which read "Here Lies the Heart of Thomas Hardy." And, I have to admit, we began to laugh.

"What it should say is 'Here Lies Thomas Hardy's Cat Cobby Inside Whom Might Lie the Heart of Thomas Hardy,'" I said.

"Or a pig's heart."

On one side of Hardy's stone was an inscription in memory of "Emma, Wife of Thomas Hardy." On the other, an inscription in memory of "Florence, Second Wife of Thomas Hardy." They were all in there together.

"It's a gravestack."

We were, of course, tired out. After the play last night, we'd stayed up later than usual talking with Anthony and Nan. They'd googled us, visited our websites, visited my daughter's website, loved Beverly's abstracted landscapes, and wanted to talk about her art. Did she paint in the field or in a studio? Some of her things, they said, called to mind

Turner, others Monet. Would she paint some Dorset scenes? And would I write about Hardy? What was Becka working on now? They insisted on a small nightcap. Then Beverly and I packed so we'd have extra time to sleep in the morning. But we woke up early anyway, had an early breakfast, said our good-byes, and were ready to begin the long, long trip back to Oregon. Just the thought of all those hours on airplanes made me loopy.

And this was our second Hardy grave, since we'd already paid our respects to his ashes in Westminster Abbey. Hardy actually had three simultaneous funerals. At two o'clock on the afternoon of January 16, 1928, there was one in Westminster Abbey, attended by his wife Florence and his sister Kate, with the prime minister among the pallbearers. A spadeful of earth from back home in Dorset had been sent along by a local farm laborer and was sprinkled on the casket. At the same hour here in Stinsford churchyard, Hardy's brother Henry led a crowd of local mourners in remembering the great author. They buried his heart in the same grave as Emma, among the tombstones of other Hardys, under a great yew tree. Also at the same hour in Dorchester all business was halted so the mayor and other notables could gather to celebrate Hardy at St. Peter's Church in Dorchester.

We were able to stop laughing when a young woman on a bicycle rode up to the churchyard gate and stopped. She removed her helmet and stashed it in the bicycle's basket, ran her fingers through her close-cropped hair, tugged her cell phone from the pocket of her pants, and stepped among the tombstones. When she found the tombstone she was looking for, she snapped a couple of pictures. Then she held the phone at arm's length and took a photo of herself before the tombstone. Studying the results made her frown.

"Sorry," she called to us, holding up the phone, wiggling it. "Selfie doesn't cut it. Would you mind taking a picture?"

Beverly was happy to help and the break gave us a chance to shake our giddiness. When we walked over I saw the name on the tombstone the woman was visiting: Cecil Day-Lewis 1904–1972 Poet Laureate.

"I didn't know he was buried here," I said.

"Brilliant, isn't it?" the woman said. "Daniel Day-Lewis's father! His mum too, right there."

Beverly snapped a photo of the woman, looked at it, moved a few steps closer so the tombstone's inscription would be clearer, and took another. She handed back the phone. "I can take more if you'd like."

The woman looked at the screen, nodded once in satisfaction, and put the phone back in her pocket. "I wonder if Daniel comes here to visit them sometime. Be ace to run into him, wouldn't it."

After she left, we sat on the bench again. Beverly lay back with her head in my lap. We looked at each other and smiled. I'd imagined seeing Hardy's grave would be a solemn, climactic moment for me. But this was turning out to be even better. I was at home with Hardy and his spirit now, his world and ours aligned in a suitably antic peace.

We were in the only place where Thomas Hardy had ever seen a ghost. He'd always wanted to see one, claimed he'd give ten years of his life for the chance. Then on Christmas Eve in 1919, at the age of seventy-nine, he was sitting here in the churchyard when a figure wearing eighteenth-century clothing appeared. It said "a green Christmas" and vanished into the church. I thought about that, and realized it too sounded like the wind. *Christmas.*

"I think the Hardy Visitations are over," I said, looking out over the family plot.

We drove out Church Lane toward the intersection with A35. It would be wide and easy all the way from there to Heathrow. At the last turn before the roundabout, I could see Dorchester in the distance. Closer, about a mile and a half from where we waited for the traffic to clear, was Max Gate. Smoke drifting above it, probably from a neighbor's chimney, was the last image I had of Hardy's home before accelerating north toward London.

"Bonfires in the garden and all," Sharon Taylor had said last night at the pub. In the weeks after his death, Florence Hardy had carried out her husband's wishes by burning his papers. The gardener had helped, raking over the ashes to be sure nothing escaped destruction. There had been other, earlier burnings in the Max Gate garden as well. Hardy had burned Emma's diaries, her writings about their marriage and about Hardy himself. He burned letters, manuscripts—including his first, unpublished novel, the one he was writing when he became involved with Tryphena.

But I don't believe he burned "Something I Missed." At eighty, shortly after the ghost in Stinsford churchyard had spoken to him of a green Christmas, Hardy wrote to a friend, "I have not been doing much—mainly destroying papers of the last thirty years & they raise ghosts." But raising ghosts was the purpose of "Something I Missed" and I believed he needed those ghosts to remain at large. As he remained at large.

In a further act of literary incineration, he'd omitted certain years and certain people from his self-ghostwritten biography (you can't find Tryphena Sparks anywhere in its 613 pages). He omitted relatives from a family tree he drew, and from his few surviving notebooks. Sure, this attempted smoke screen looked bad, even incriminating. The bonfires might as well be signal flares announcing that there was something to hide. Hardy could live—and could die—with that. Because "Something I Missed" remained.

Hardy was far from the only writer to have torched the record. Charles Dickens did it, at least twice, and wished he'd been able to find every letter he'd written so he could add them to the fire. Henry James did it too, including one famous burn that consumed forty years' worth of manuscripts and notebooks and letters. Samuel Johnson, Sigmund Freud. In the end, none of these writers could truly control the way their stories were told or the conclusions drawn. That part of the afterlife is in the hands of the living, and its narrative is always an act of hypothesis.

For all that, I still didn't believe Hardy burned "Something I Missed." It had to survive him. The problem was what to do with it.

The road curved toward the northeast. We passed a sign showing Puddletown straight ahead. To the left was the turnoff for Cuckoo Lane.

We stopped at a gas station near Heathrow for a fill-up. Beverly went into the small market and bought a tube of superglue. As I topped off the tank, she knelt beside the ravaged front left tire and glued the flaps of rubber back in place.

"I know it won't last," she said. "But I had to try. It just looked so sad."

When we returned the car at the Avis lot, an attendant came over to inspect it. He checked the dashboard and noted we'd driven 1,512 miles.

"Enjoy your travels?" he asked.

"Very much," I said, and knew at once I'd said too much.

Hearing my American accent, he knew what to do. He walked directly to the left front of the car. He crouched to study the tire and wheel, touched them, made a few notes on his clipboard, and stood up. "Did you hit a pothole?"

It cost us £135. We'd thought it would surely be more than that.

16

The night we got home to Portland, I had trouble sleeping. After a restless hour, I got out of bed and walked to the front of our home to see the river shimmer in the full moon's light. I thought that something in the way current and reflected clouds worked on the river's shifting surface would settle me down, tell me for sure where I was. I saw driftwood flicker on the bank. Almost lost in shadow, a sailboat rocked at anchor near Ross Island's north tip. From time to time, because I knew they must be there, I saw the great blue heron nests clustered at the top of the cottonwoods. I thought if my body knew I was home, sleep would come. But when Beverly called to me from bed, I knew I'd gotten up only to return to her.

There's a moment early in *Jude the Obscure* when young Jude Fawley sees the city of Christminster for the first time. It's twenty miles away, revealing itself in sundown light after a long day trapped in mist. Christminster—Hardy's stand-in for Oxford—strikes the orphaned country lad as a bejeweled vision, with points of light gleaming like the topaz.

To see this sight, Jude has walked two or three gloomy miles from his great-aunt's bakery in the hamlet of Marygreen to a hilltop vantage point. He imagines Christminster as a magical place full of books he yearns to read and scholarship he yearns to join.

Though men of Jude's class had no chance of admission, what drives him is a touching, innocent, utterly absurd fantasy of becoming a son of the university and, by doing so, raising himself from his humble background. It's a glorious dream of education's power, and by the time I read this scene, in the last of Hardy's novels, in the last months of my transformative undergraduate years, under the guidance of my beloved mentor, I felt myself to be fully there with Jude.

I was moved by Jude's—and Hardy's—passion for education, the belief in what occurs behind those brick walls, within those brick buildings, in the pages of books and the mind opened to the world by knowledge.

I wasn't an orphan, came from a family of butchers rather than masons, but I'd been fatherless since the age of fourteen and yearned to get away from the small apartment where I ended up living with my desperately unhappy mother. There weren't necessarily points of light gleaming like the topaz in Lancaster, Pennsylvania, or on the campus of Franklin and Marshall College during my time there. In fact, the most noticeable effect was the odor of tobacco from the Hess and Millysack cigar factories nearby. But the place, which I came to with no idea of what I was seeking, took me in at a crucial moment in my life, brought Robert Russell and then Thomas Hardy into my life, and allowed me to find my life's work. Exactly as the dream of an education, as Jude's dream, was supposed to work, though it didn't for Jude.

Now the team had reunited and expanded. Again with no idea what I was seeking other than to offer homage to Thomas Hardy and the recently deceased Robert Russell, I was allowed to discover something I'd missed about Hardy. With Beverly by my side and fully in my heart, with Hardy Visiting me and Russell there for me, I'd reached a kind of understanding about the writer whose work and life haunted me for nearly half a century. He'd hoped to shield himself from suffering the pain of losing love by turning away from love. But it didn't work and he knew it didn't work. This was an even deeper suffering, because he could neither stop falling in love nor stay in love, and it took him more than a lifetime to see that what we learn from such suffering is what makes us most capable of love. I think now that I always knew this about Hardy. I just didn't know I knew it.

Along the way, a quest emerged in which the chance to make sense of Hardy's strangeness and struggle gave me a chance to make sense of my own. I was engaged in an ongoing process of learning to live as a brain-damaged man and resist neurological disintegration.

Once we got home from England, I began to read and reread Hardy. All I knew was that, as I told Beverly only moments after Hardy had touched and spoken to me in front of Barclays Bank in Dorchester, Hardy had passed a story to me, a book whose pages as yet had no words. I would have to write the true story of the Visitations. All of them, including the last one, including what I'd seen there.

Even if there were no such book as "Something I Missed," the truth of Robert Russell's and Thomas Hardy's legacy to me had been revealed: the struggle to speak from the heart—even if in the end Hardy failed to be able to speak fully, even if he failed to be heard—was what mattered most. Such speaking was a form of self-surrender, an end to withholding, a risk. But it was self-surrender that paradoxically allowed for self-survival.

I remembered Nan Swain saying, as we sat with her and Anthony over tea at their B&B, that people want to see Hardy so badly they somehow manage to succeed. She was right, as Beverly was right. I'd wanted to see Hardy. Seeing him, and engaging in the search for what he missed, fulfilled a deep need—too long postponed—to express in action my grief over Russell's death, and my love and gratitude for how these men had repeatedly helped me speak.

I read eight biographies of Hardy, along with Lois Deacon's book of sordid allegations and Robert Gittings's demolition of its claims, discovering that each writer revealed a sometimes slightly / sometimes vastly different Thomas Hardy. Each had a different view of Emma, of Tryphena, of Hardy's marriages and romances, of events and their meaning. I read Emma's recollections, books of Hardy criticism and letters, and books about the landscape of his work. The thing that most writers agree about is Hardy's essential secrecy. This could mean he had awful things to hide but it also could mean he didn't want to be known except by his work. And in the end, there was work he didn't want known too. Until he did. Until his restless spirit cried out for the work to be seen.

There's no consensus. There never is and never can be. There are, instead, stories. Some more credible than others.

$$\maltese$$

I can't tell you how many times I looked at the photographs Beverly had taken while we were in Dorset. We had them loaded onto her computer and we also uploaded them to a lab that printed them out. For months as I read all those books, I kept returning to the photos, making notes, writing scenes and descriptions in my journal. I kept studying the images, in particular, of places where Hardy had appeared to me— South Street in Dorchester, the bedroom at his cottage in Bockhampton, the Nut Walk and study at Max Gate. I found additional images of these places online too.

Since I kept our photos in chronological order, and since the ones from the Nut Walk and the Pet Cemetery were together, I got caught up in looking at the tombstones. It was only possible to identify a few of the names. Some were fully clear—Wessex, Moss, Comfy, Chips—and some partially clear. Even with a magnifying glass, or with the zoom feature on our computer, I couldn't make out all the pets' names, and it seemed like the engraving on some of the stones had eroded away. Some stones had sunk into the grass. I wanted to identify as many of the pets as I could, get their names and stories into what I was writing. It was driving me crazy.

One clear afternoon in late fall, when the sunlight over the river was most intense and shining into our living room, Beverly was at her computer and I was sitting on the couch nearby holding the photos up one-by-one to have yet another look. We both wore baseball hats as usual to shield our eyes from the glare, and mine was my lucky Brooklyn Dodgers hat. In a close-up shot of the very southern edge of the Pet Cemetery, on one of the semisunken stones, in the brilliant beam of sunlight coming through our windows, I thought I saw some letters I hadn't been able to make out before. Or rather, had taken for shadows before. I didn't want to move.

"Can you bring over the magnifying glass?"

Beverly and I traded the magnifying glass back and forth. As the light shifted, so did we, keeping the photo aglow.

"Shadows?" I asked.

"Across the top, maybe. But on the stone's face I think there are two, maybe three letters."

"I do too."

"This is amazing."

"Tell me what you see."

"R. U." She stopped. "Can't be sure, but it sure looks like there's a B too. And there's room for one more letter if the engraver centered the name."

"I know the names of eight Hardy pets. None were named Ruby."

⚬

We'd been keeping in e-mail contact with Jason Abbott III. He'd begun sending along chapters of his work on *Love's Geometry*, which was now subtitled *The Secret Formula of Relationship in the Novels of Thomas Hardy*. He'd also been telling us about his own relationship, no longer secret or geometrical, with Katie Pole Crosbie.

He was surprised when we wrote that we'd solved that equation months earlier, after seeing them together on the night of the play. But he was even more surprised when we wrote about what might be buried under a stone in the Pet Cemetery.

I told him I had a theory that Hardy had written and hidden a novel. Told him what I thought it was about, and why I believed Hardy had written and hidden it. Though he knew I had neurological issues, I saw no reason to tell him about my Visitations. Just suggesting there was a hidden book manuscript was nutty enough already. I hoped he didn't dismiss my theory as just another kind of brain misfire.

I didn't need to spell out why—if I were correct and Jason found it—"Something I Missed" and its story of the love between Patrick Stone and Ruby Heartsfield would be a career-making discovery for him. Jason didn't press me to reveal how I'd come up with the book's title or the main characters' names. Within ten minutes he confirmed that the stone, sunken and badly eroded, did contain the faintly etched name Ruby. And that there had been no pets that bore the name Ruby.

⇶

In his fourteen published novels, Thomas Hardy had said all he *wanted* to say. That's what he told the inquiring journalist in 1906 and that still rings true. But in his hidden, secret novel, Hardy tried to say what he *had* to say. And eighty-four years after his death, he appeared ready for that secret to emerge.

The day after he'd opened the grave, Jason and I spoke by Skype. He was at the desk in his upstairs bedroom. Through the door behind him I could see the hallway Beverly and I had walked along when we were at Max Gate. He held up before the screen what he'd found buried in the Pet Cemetery, a thick stack of paper.

"A manuscript all right," he said. "Four hundred and seventeen handwritten pages. Elaborately wrapped and secured. Very little damage to the paper. Handwriting looks like Hardy's, no question. But Hardy on speed. Quite a mess."

"Can you read it?"

"Already have. It's unfinished, breaks off in midsentence with no resolution in sight. Guess what the last two words are."

"Love is . . . ," I said.

"I missed . . . ," Beverly said.

"No rest," Jason said.

Then he held up the book's title page. I wasn't sure it was Hardy's handwriting—I'm no expert—but seeing the inked script was haunting. This was a page that had been written calmly:

Something I Missed:
A Novel of Love
Found and Lost
and Mourned
By
Thomas Hardy

There were legal matters to deal with, and forensic work to rule out forgery, to establish that the manuscript was in Hardy's hand, written on paper and with ink that would have been available to him between, say, 1890, when Tryphena died and the writing most likely began, and 1928, when Hardy died. The National Trust would be brought in, the Dorset County Museum and the Hardy Society. International scholars. But Jason assured me he would follow through and keep me posted.

"It's Hardy," he said. "Most likely a second or third draft. Even so, all marked up with corrections. Still reads with the intensity of a first draft."

We spoke for a few more minutes about logistics. Then Jason glanced at his watch and said he had to go. "An unknown Hardy novel," he added just before signing off. "It is, as you Americans say, a game changer."

"You know what, Jason? I feel like I've already read it."

Hardy had said, "No rest." But maybe now there would be rest.

⸙

Until Becka suggested it, I'd never thought of trying to track down the surviving copy of my college thesis on Hardy. "Since I was a kid you've been talking about Thomas Hardy. And your thesis."

When she said that, I instantly saw her sitting on a brown shag rug in the living room of our home in Springfield, Illinois. Given that rug, and the floral-patterned green and yellow hide-a-bed couch behind her, and the moving boxes stacked against a wall, the year had to be 1973. Late autumn, as we were still settling in to the rented house on South Glenwood. So Becka was just one year old in that moment. Smiling, wearing her grandmother's fox-fur earmuffs, she held my Hardy thesis open across her knees, pretending to be halfway through reading it.

If nothing else, Becka pointed out, getting hold of the thesis would further establish continuity with myself as I was then. With Robert Russell too and with my initial and therefore essential reactions to Hardy. And wasn't all that, especially reconnecting with the past, what my work had been about since I got sick in 1988? Isn't it why I went to Dorset?

It seemed impossible that anyone could find one forty-four-year-old thesis among 225 years' worth of Franklin and Marshall College theses. No way. To locate it, I thought, would require so many steps to have been taken successfully in the past: "To Christminster: A Study of the Development of the Novels of Thomas Hardy" would have had to go from the English Department offices to the college library to some shelf somewhere in that building and to wherever it was stored when the library had been extensively remodeled fourteen years after I graduated. It would have had to come back to the library again, perhaps been copied in some electronic manner, and followed through generations of tracking-system updates. Among all the other theses in every department throughout all those years.

That night, I had a version of the dream I have two or three times a year. I'm wandering the familiar campus of Franklin and Marshall College, feeling at once deeply at home and completely lost. Landmarks—Old Main, Hartman Oval, the twin water towers, the gnarled Protest Tree before the bookstore entrance—are not in the right places. Buildings are oriented in strange ways. The baseball field on which I played for the freshman team was located where the Green Room Theatre should be. I'm late for class, can't find the right room though I know where it's located, don't have the books I need.

The next morning, I sent e-mails to some friends at Franklin and Marshall asking for suggestions about locating my thesis. They put me in touch with the Information Literacy Librarian, who put me in touch with her College Archives colleagues, one of whom sent me two PDF files, each containing half of my thesis. The process had taken just under twenty-four hours. They wrote to say they were able to make a copy from the original onion-skin paper, and then scan into searchable PDF documents.

By now, it's surely not a surprise to know what happened next. I cried.

⁂

In the introduction to my thesis, I'd said I was "attempting to establish a sense of unmistakable continuity in Hardy's work as a novelist, with a view of each novel in terms of its relationship to the ones that precede it." At the end of such investigation, I declared, "it will be possible to judge the total performance of creative genius with clearer insight."

Not quite, Floyd, eh? But forty-four years later, and after three days in Dorset, you're a little closer. To Hardy and to yourself. And that, I feel, is what the encounter with a great writer, a writer struggling to speak, to say what he's trying to say, is supposed to do.

It was Russell who put me together with Hardy and brought that issue into focus, connecting Hardy's struggle to speak with my own. "This is it, you know," he had said to me. And I'd needed to hear him then, in 1968, when I was first finding my voice as a person and writer, and I needed to hear him again in 1988, when I was silenced by illness, and I needed to hear him once more, after he had died and I was in search of "something I missed."

⁂

I'd spent the day reading my thesis and rereading key passages it led me to in some of Hardy's novels. I'd also been rereading Robert Russell's autobiography, its yellowed and densely printed pages now detached from the binding so that I held each one in my hand as I read it. My eyes felt strained, my head muddled.

Around six o'clock that evening, as I began dicing red peppers and Kalamata olives to go with the broccolini and feta cheese, Beverly said, "That looks good."

When I glanced over toward the couch to smile at her, bright light from the reading lamp tilted above her head made my vision explode. Just a quirk of the angles. A sudden flash of light is the most frequent trigger for my migraines, which always last about twenty minutes and follow a predictable course. Already I could see a blazing yellow hole open up in my vision field and begin to fill with sharp, sizzling images, a dazzle of toothy Picasso-esque jagged pieces flickering faster and faster.

I put down my knife, took off my glasses, and stood stock-still. The air seemed to pulsate. I could see Beverly, but I could also now see a sequence of black and yellow interlocking gears churning between us. There was a green and red flickering off to the south as though the room was filling with hummingbirds. Seeing me frozen in place, eyes open but unfocused, Beverly understood at once what was happening and came to help me over to the couch.

"I'll get the feverfew tincture," she said, and walked toward our bedroom.

Alone on the couch, I kept my eyes closed. That was my usual way of dealing with the intense part of these attacks. It wouldn't stop the flow of forms but at least the migraine's visual chaos wouldn't be competing with perceptions of the room around me or of the darkening skies. Locked into a view that included only pure disturbance—optical static—I looked around that inner space and decided to reject it. No, I will not dwell in that, will not close myself off inside its strangeness. I realized that what I wanted most was to let the outside world in too, let it coexist with the crazed emanations from within my flaring brain and optic nerve.

I knew these distortions would soon begin to fade and the visions become a memory—if I made a note about it. They were just another part of the story, another kind of Visitation.

I opened my eyes. The off-white ceiling, the track lights, the water sprinklers in their cozy cages, wavered above me. A glimmer like light off the river below could have been as real as the sunset or could have been a symptom of misperception. I heard Beverly approaching before I saw her. Then she was beside me, a cup of feverfew in her hand, smiling, helping me sit up.

It was just before the winter solstice, a few weeks after our Skype visit with Jason. He'd sent an e-mail saying he was working to authenticate "Something I Missed." But for now its existence was a secret shared by us and what he called "a few trusted allies on a need-to-know basis." There had been no public announcement yet. I appreciated his scholarly caution, his sense of responsibility, and was glad he was in control of the manuscript going forward. I felt it would be Jason's job eventually to tell the story of Hardy's unfinished novel and define its position and properties in the author's geometry of love. I had a different story to tell.

All the reading I'd been doing since we got home from England, the notes I'd been collecting in their color-coded file folders, the photographs and conversations with Beverly or Becka about what had happened in Dorset, had left me confused about how to begin the story I had to tell. My desk looked migrainous.

Shortly after noon, as we shared an omelet, Beverly and I talked about the year that was nearing an end. In 2012 I'd turned sixty-five, she'd turned sixty, and we'd been together twenty years. We'd celebrated each of those milestones. Part of that celebration had been finally getting to England, and having those last three days in Hardy country.

"I think I know what we need to do," Beverly said. "We need a ceremony for what happened there. We need to honor it. And then I know you'll be ready to tell your story."

I put down my fork, wiped my mouth, and tried not to cry.

"What kind of ceremony?"

She smiled at me and shrugged. "Why don't you just start gathering things. Let's see what happens."

I was surprised by the immediate rush of clarity. Over the half year since we'd gotten home I'd failed to give thanks for what had happened in Dorset. Failed to express gratitude for the opportunity it gave me to acknowledge how Robert Russell and Thomas Hardy affect my life. For how much I had learned about myself as well as about Hardy. All I'd been doing was worrying about how to explain it. But now I knew exactly what I wanted to gather, knew exactly where I wanted to place it all, and knew exactly when the ceremony should occur.

I spread a piece of cloth on the couch, placing it where I'd been sitting when sunlight flooded into the room and revealed Ruby's name in the photo I'd been holding. Over the next two hours, I selected items and brought them to the cloth, carrying only one at a time, savoring the process of assembling the ceremony's pieces, the integration of each into the whole.

By the time the sun reached the couch, Beverly and I were sitting there with the cloth between us. It held my copy of *To Catch an Angel*, the pages kept in place by a rubber band. It held a copy of *Jude the Obscure*, the novel of Hardy's that once restored my hope in finding a way back from illness. I'd photocopied Hardy's poem about Tryphena, written after he learned of her death, where he'd called her "my lost prize" and said, "I do but the phantom retain." Online I'd found an image of heath-ponies and printed it out. At the center of the cloth was a collage of photographs: the Barclays Bank building in Dorchester (home of the Mayor of Casterbridge, where Hardy's mingled real and imagined worlds first appeared to us and where the Visitations began), images of Hardy, Emma, Tryphena, the room where Hardy was born at Bockhampton, Hardy's study, Emma's attic room, the Nut Walk, and the Pet Cemetery at Max Gate. There was a photograph of our five Dorset friends taken at the pub after we'd watched the play, Jason and Katie leaning together with their glasses raised, Anthony and Nan holding hands, Sharon scribbling notes on her paper napkin. There was a photograph of Beverly and me standing at the cliff's edge overlooking Durdle Door as the wind blew. And because she'd been in my mind and heart all during the trip, been an inspiration to pursue the story wherever it led, there was a photograph of my daughter.

Beverly and I sat together holding hands over the cloth and feeling the December sun warm on our backs as it also drenched the items I'd assembled. We closed our eyes for a few minutes.

"This is good," I said. I opened my eyes and studied the items on the cloth. "I can feel things beginning to fall into place."

"When we decided to go to Dorset, what did you think would happen?"

"That I'd pay my respects and be done with Thomas Hardy."

"Didn't happen that way, did it?"

I shook my head. "Clearly, I'm not done with Thomas Hardy. Or, fortunately, with Robert Russell." I thought about the chaos on my writing desk. "Not even close."

From outside, we could hear the piercing screech of killdeer from a field just to our south. At this hour, they must be spooked by someone's off-leash dog. I recognized their trill of terror that meant they were trying to lead intruders from their nesting ground, even though nesting season had passed.

"Do you hear that?" Beverly asked.

"Killdeer."

"Listen when the killdeer are quiet."

That's when I began to hear another, softer sound. A vaguely familiar piping.

"What is that?"

"A flock of juvenile white-crowned sparrows. They're practicing, trying to master their songs."

⪦

On a bookshelf beside my desk I keep collections of poetry I can't do without. These books are so essential to me that I have to be able to see and reach them when I sit here. They're talismans as well as books that I take down and refer to urgently. Of course Thomas Hardy is there, taking up one and three-quarters inches of precious space. Robert Frost is there, T. S. Eliot, Thomas Kinsella, Elizabeth Bishop. But the only other book comparable in size to the Hardy is Robert Lowell's *Collected Poems*. That's why, when I reached for the Hardy without focusing my attention on the shelf, I ended up pulling the Lowell down instead. It was late on a March afternoon, we'd been home from England for nine months, and I could feel throughout my body that the time had come to write this book. Enough work had been read, enough notes taken, alternative titles for my book sorted out. My brain, so easily over-whelmed when there were competing stimuli, or when it was asked to establish structure, organize, think abstractly, felt close to crashing.

I plopped the Lowell book on my desk. It fell open to page 838, where the spine has long been cracked. The poem facing me was titled "Epilogue," and as I read it I felt certain that Thomas Hardy had inter-vened once again, ducked aside to make sure I picked up Lowell this time. Smack in the middle of "Epilogue" I came to the line I needed in order to begin: "Why not say what happened?"

Well: Beverly and I walked up South Street in Dorchester, following a tourist map past Trespass Outdoor Clothing, Carphone Warehouse, Top Drawer Cards & Gifts, a shuttered O2 Store.

Acknowledgments

My wife, Beverly Hallberg, lived this book with me. She supported and encouraged me through all four drafts, and has long shown me that to love is to speak the heart.

My daughter, Rebecca Skloot, has enriched my life and spirit from the instant I held her in my arms in the first moments after her birth. Now my colleague and friend too, a guiding spirit and example, she knew what this book needed to be before I did.

My friends Herman Asarnow, Christine Sneed, Ron Slate, and Emma Sweeney read drafts and offered valuable comments.

I found the following biographies most helpful while working on this novel: Claire Tomalin's *Thomas Hardy* (2007), Ralph Pite's *Thomas Hardy: The Guarded Life* (2006), Michael Millgate's *Thomas Hardy: A Biography Revisited* (2004), Martin Seymour-Smith's *Hardy* (1994), Robert Gittings's *Young Thomas Hardy* (1975) and *Thomas Hardy's Later Years* (1978), Timothy O'Sullivan's *Thomas Hardy: An Illustrated Biography* (1975), and *The Early Life of Thomas Hardy, 1840–1891* and *The Later Years of Thomas Hardy, 1892–1928*, written by Thomas Hardy but published under Florence Hardy's name. Emma Hardy's *Recollections* (1961), along with Lois Deacon and Terry Coleman's *Providence and Mr. Hardy* (1962), were essential background documents to the Hardy story, and Tony Fincham's *Hardy's Landscape Revisited* (2010) and J. B. Bullen's *Thomas Hardy: The World of His Novels* (2013) helped shape my appreciation of the Dorset setting.